PLUNDERING THE PLANETARY SECRETS

THE FORGOTTEN PLANET

BOOK 2

KATE MACLEOD

CHAPTER 1

A month ago, Lafayette Eloi would have sworn she'd never find a less welcoming setting than the dense, muddy jungle her father had brought her to. That was after she had left the only home she had ever known, a village in the grasslands of the southern end of the Great Grassy Sea.

Lafayette was sure if anyone besides the two of them had laid eyes on that jungle, it had been centuries before. Maybe even longer. Because that jungle had filled the crater around the fallen ship her father had worked his entire life to find.

She, along with her mother's dog Kora, had spent a few weeks there alone in a campsite situated in as much of a clearing as those trees provided. The almost daily rain—paired with the overlapping branches of the tree canopy high above that kept out all but the smallest amount of sunlight—had made for a landscape that was always wet and filled with unpleasant smells.

Along with the annoying preponderance of insects and the more dangerous presence of cat-like predators with glider wings that haunted the treetops—and all too frequently, the tree bottoms as well —the grind of just keeping her feet moving through the heavy, boot-sucking mud had made even the shortest of journeys a real slog.

But now Lafayette was back in a grassland. But it wasn't like the grassland she knew from home. This was the unique version of grassland that surrounded the capital city.

And it was, if anything, worse than that jungle.

OK. There was no sucking mud here. It had that going for it.

But the grasses around her here and now were of no type she had ever seen before. The village that had been her childhood home had been surrounded by cultivated grains. But further west, closer to the jungle-filled crater, she had seen wild grasses that had been inedible, but still of a grainy type that looked familiar to her. And for the first part of her journey towards the capital city from the lip of that crater, those same wild grasses had prevailed.

Yet what was dancing all around her now in the stiff, hot breeze was entirely alien to her experience. Although surely her mother must have known it. Her mother had spent years in the capital. And yet, search her mother's journals as she might, Lafayette hadn't found a single mention of what it was she was looking at now.

It was entirely possible this grass was so ordinary to her mother's experience it wouldn't even have occurred to her that anyone would wonder about it.

Lafayette would never really know. Her mother had died before Lafayette even knew this would be a thing she'd liked to have asked.

It felt like a million years ago, the day she had buried her mother among the roots of the tree at the heart of their village.

But it had only been two months. Only a little longer than since she had lost her dad. Although he wasn't dead. He was just… gone.

But Lafayette tried not to think about that. Mostly she failed, but she always tried. She tried to keep her mind anchored in this strange new world around her.

The grass here was taller than any Lafayette had ever seen. It was so tall that even the man she could see a few paces ahead of her standing on top of his wheeled caravan wagon to gaze around couldn't see over the tops of that grass. And yet it wasn't woody like bamboo.

Not that Lafayette had ever seen bamboo, only the sketches in her mother's carefully detailed style in her journal. But the sketches were intricate, fully rendered in color, and all the significant features were labeled in her mother's flowing script. And Lafayette had nearly memorized every page of her mother's journal. She would know bamboo if she saw it now.

No, these grasses grew out of the ground in blades as thick around as Lafayette's thigh. But despite that girth, they maintained edges sharp enough to cut the unwary. And their sap was an irritant. Some people were more reactive to it than others, but Lafayette had seen enough slow-healing wounds on fellow travelers to not want to test her own reaction. She strove to keep herself among the wary. She wore her long-sleeved shirts and canvas pants despite the oppressive heat, and she never ventured out of her tent without her boots protecting her feet.

But the possibility of infected cuts was far from the only danger the grass posed to travelers. In fact, it wasn't even the chief one.

The clumps of the grass were dense, sprouting so close together that those enormous blades would interweave into something like mats, albeit mats with cutting edges it was best to avoid.

It certainly seemed to be impossible to cross that terrain without a lot of work with a scythe or a machete to clear the path before you. And fire would be better. Which was why most travelers stuck to the roads.

And yet, somehow, bandits still found a way to melt into all that green and lie in wait for, again, the unwary. They could slip out of that tangled mass of sharp-edged grass, strike wayward travelers for whatever they wanted to have for themselves, then melt back into the green without so much as a trace of their passing left behind them.

Lafayette didn't know how they did it. But she'd come across more than one wagon left burned out and abandoned on the side of the road. A few had still been smoldering.

So she did what all travelers did who weren't either members of the patrolling law enforcers or weren't themselves traders so wealthy they could afford to hire ex-patrolling law enforcers for their personal security force.

She traveled with as many other people as she could in a caravan of wagons.

Because there was safety in numbers.

But for Lafayette and her late mother's dog Kora, there was also danger in crowds.

So Lafayette tried to have it both ways. She made sure the two of them walked at the back of the line, staying close enough to huddle in for protection if bandits did make an appearance, but as apart as it was reasonable to be from overly curious eyes during the endless days of slow, trudging walking over the dry but fissured and cracked dirt surface of the roads.

Lafayette didn't mind the drudgery. She was good at keeping up a steady pace, one foot in front of the other for as long as it takes.

But lately, she didn't like the way two of the caravan kids in particular kept staring at her and Kora.

Well, mostly Kora.

Kora was a dog, but she wasn't the only dog in the caravan. Lots of the family wagons had a dog or two as part of the group. And some of the others were even part of the patrolling watch that kept an eye out for trouble.

Or, in the case of the dogs, kept their keen hearing and sense of smell attuned for signs of trouble.

But Kora was from the capital originally, and Lafayette had hoped that the long, reddish fur that needed daily brushing to stay neat and free of burrs wouldn't look so out of place as she got closer to the city. Because it always had, back in Lafayette's home village.

But, alas, the other dogs in the caravan were all shades of brown or gray, lanky where Kora was rounder, their tails more rat-like than Kora's curled up fluff of orange and white waves of hair.

And maybe that's all it was that was drawing those children's eyes to her. That she was different. That she was a handsome dog.

But Lafayette could never let herself trust that that was all it was.

Because under the woven mat of dried grass that Lafayette had made herself for Kora to wear, the dog's middle section was all metal. She had machines inside her body that kept her alive after she should've died from a combination of old age and grief at Lafayette's mother's passing.

Kora had always been Lafayette's mother's dog. At the time just after the surgery, Lafayette hadn't been entirely easy in her mind with what her father had done.

He had thought fixing Kora was a kindness to Lafayette, already grieving her mother. But Kora had only wanted to lie down and rest next to the remains of her best friend.

Metal was rare, and machines were rarer still. But they weren't unheard of. Still, seeing Kora moving around again had unnerved Lafayette's neighbors enough that it had been just as well Lafayette chose to leave with her father and never go back.

But even as she got closer to the capital, most of the wagons in the caravan around her were still rolling on wheels, not floating on hover discs. Most had engines that drove the axles, but there were a few closer to the back being pulled by oxen.

Kora, with her metal body, didn't fit in here any more than she had back home. So Lafayette kept her covered up. The parts that kept her alive were all things that people would understand if she explained them to the curious lookers on. But those questions might lead to other questions. Questions about her father.

Questions she absolutely did not want to get into. At least not until she'd had a conversation with her father's mentor in the capital city. She needed his advice on what she could say and what had to stay secret.

Because she was really afraid that almost all of it would be safer kept secret.

But more than just keeping her organs alive, Kora also had another, very different kind of machine inside her. One that contained something called a construct—a ghostly yet somehow living thing—of a schoolteacher that Lafayette had rescued from the fallen ship before it had taken off back into space.

The construct she had saved when she hadn't been able to save her own father. He was still trapped on that ship, trapped up in space, where every night Lafayette could watch the dot of light that was him crossing the sky.

That construct was something Lafayette was sure none of these people had ever seen before. She would bet anything that even in the capital city itself, it would attract attention. Even though it couldn't project as an image anymore, it could talk through Kora. And that was impossible to explain away as just part of her robot half. A robot was a machine. A construct was something so much more.

Keeping it secret was paramount. The only thing that mattered more was getting to the capital city alive. Which meant dealing with the presence of others.

Lafayette had covered every bit of metal across Kora's mid section with that grass mat so as not to draw curious eyes or attract uncomfortable questions.

But she had also rigged two packs together into a pair of saddlebags of sorts, and Kora carried those as they walked. Not that Lafayette couldn't have fit everything in her own wheelbarrow. But it helped explained the grass mat as something like a saddle blanket. And, what with the hover disc keeping her belly up off the ground so that her paws barely needed to carry her weight, Kora didn't mind the weight.

Still, those two kids had been looking Kora's way far too often over the last few days. Lafayette didn't like it. If they had seen a glint of metal, wouldn't they just have assumed it was from one of the pack buckles or something?

The two kids were siblings, riding in the same caravan wagon when they weren't walking. And they had the same tattered short pants from too many close passes to the blades of grass at the sides of the road, the same shapeless short-sleeved tunics in mottled shades of green.

The same bowl-like haircut. Honestly, if they were brothers, sisters, or one of each, it was impossible for Lafayette to tell.

But they had the same piercing green eyes. The eyes that were always silently watching.

And Lafayette just couldn't shake the feeling that something was about to happen.

Of course she was right about that. She had to be. It was the way the world worked.

It was always only a matter of time before something *had* to happen. It was just a question of when.

And from what direction it would come.

CHAPTER 2

Lafayette was just slowing her steps so she and Kora could fall a little bit further behind, away from those kids, when she felt in her bones more than heard with her ears a hush settle over the entire caravan.

Then she saw hands raise up and fists close—the signal to hunker down and be silent—rippling its way down the caravan line.

Lafayette gently set down the handles of her wheelbarrow and took a step closer to Kora. And regretted she no longer had her father's shock stick. Not that she could do much with it. It would knock a person down, but just one. Still, she would've felt better just having something in her hands.

She wanted to ask if Kora sensed anything. She could see the dog's ears shifting. She could hear the snuffling sound of her nose scenting the air.

But, even if Lafayette wanted to risk a quick exchange of words, Kora was terrible at whispering.

So Lafayette held her tongue and relied on her own senses for the moment. She swept her gaze all around them, and tried to do the same with her ears and nose.

The blades of grass curved over the road, not quite enough to make a tunnel of green over the rutted path, but enough to make the air feel close. Humid. She could hear the breeze that rustled through the tops of the grass, making the blades scrape together in a way that almost sounded like singing. But she couldn't feel it. It didn't reach her. There wasn't the faintest stirring of air to cool the heat of her sweaty skin.

Then Lafayette realized that, as much as the humans and dogs around her had gone quiet on command, the insects she should be hearing droning all around them were silent as well.

Despite the heat, she felt an icy chill run up her spine. Maybe it wasn't a false alarm this time. As large as their caravan was, maybe this particular group of bandits were numerous enough to feel confident in taking them despite the patrollers visibly carrying rifles and needle guns.

Or worse, these bandits were desperate enough to try anyway. In which case, even if they failed and were driven off, people were going to get hurt.

People always got hurt.

Lafayette dropped to one knee and put an arm around Kora's neck. Kora leaned into her as if grateful for the comforting gesture. Which was ironic, since Lafayette had done it so that Kora could comfort her.

But they were in this together. And that was its own comfort.

The seconds ticked by, only the drip of sweat down Lafayette's back marking the time. The members of the caravan who were walking the patrol peered into the impenetrable green of the grasslands, taking careful steps in their soft-soled shoes that made no sound at all. They exchanged looks with each other and occasionally another hand sign or two. Questions and answers.

But mostly they exchanged shakes of their heads.

Then, again starting somewhere in the front of the train, the sound of murmuring voices returned, followed by rattles and clanks as all the different wagons and carts got back underway.

"False alarm," someone—an older man—grumbled from somewhere up ahead of Lafayette. "Another false alarm."

"Better than the alternative," a woman grumbled back at him. But she had pitched her voice even lower than his.

Lafayette made one last attempt to stare further than three meters into the grass around the road, but had to give it up as fruitless. She couldn't see a thing. Whatever had just almost happened would have to remain a mystery to her.

But with the way the insects had gone silent, something had definitely been close. Maybe not bandits. Maybe a lone traveler who didn't like the look of their caravan. Or maybe some sort of animal. But something had been out there. Something had been watching them with purpose. And then that something had slunk away.

"Come on, Kora," Lafayette said as she bent to pick up the handles of her wheelbarrow.

Kora said nothing. But she wagged her curl of a tail, then fell into step beside Lafayette. If there was something a little too jaunty in her trotting steps, Lafayette didn't have the heart to tell her to plod more.

Lafayette was plodding enough for both of them. Kora, with all the gray from her previous old age thoroughly gone from her lush red hair after becoming half-robot, looked puppy-like enough to explain her ceaseless energy.

But those kids were still watching from the back of the wagon in front of Lafayette. And their unwavering attention was starting to edge Lafayette's annoyance over into real anger.

If they had questions, they should just come out and ask. Staring was rude.

And she really didn't want to know what came after the staring failed to satisfy their curiosity.

There were no more false alarms, although sunset had faded to a barest hint of indigo to the west before they reached the roughly maintained clearing of chopped down grass that was their designated campsite.

Lafayette parked her wheelbarrow outside the ring of caravan wagons, and Kora looked up at her with a question in her dark brown eyes.

Lafayette said nothing. She just set about unpacking and putting up her little tent.

The roomy tent she had started her journey with was long gone, traded for this smaller tent just big enough for her and Kora to curl up in together. The family she had traded with had given her what, at the time, had felt like an enormous quantity of lentils and rice to make up the difference. And she had run out of food stores the day she had left the crater behind. It had been a necessary trade, and one of her first ones.

But every bit of those lentils and rice was gone now. Necessitating more trades. Like the shock stick. And the perimeter fence. Then all the shovels and tools of her father's archaeology trade.

Then finally as many of the artifacts her father had spent his entire life collecting as she could safely part with.

She didn't need any of it. Not really. But some of it wasn't safe to sell. Because, as always, it might lead to questions. Questions she couldn't answer. She truly didn't know where most of it had come from. Or what it could do besides be reshaped to some new but more rudimentary purpose.

Although his journals held clues. Which was why the journals were safely wrapped in tattered, old grass mats, lining the bottoms of all the containers she used to store her clothes and bedding, her cooking utensils and food supplies, and her tent. She didn't dare touch those journals, not even on a night like this when she was cooking her own dinner by her tent pitched far from the rest of the camp.

Well, especially not this night.

She still felt eyes on her. Probably those two kids, although she didn't look around to find out. She just kept her gaze focused on her own tasks. Pitching the tent. Cooking her food. Brushing the dirt of the road out of Kora's coat. Checking the wheel of her wheelbarrow for signs of damage.

After Lafayette had traded the more mundanely useful, less cryptic-looking of her father's artifacts for food and with the large tent long since gone, there had been really no reason to keep the hover cart anymore. And traveling with this caravan hadn't been free.

She could still see her father's hover cart, nearer the bonfire in the center of camp where most of the people of the caravan were gathering. It carried two enormous water tanks now, often necessary when traveling through the drier parts of the grasslands. In exchange for the cart, Lafayette got a share of that water and the safety of the armed caravan patrols. Plus some more food rations, which were now almost gone.

Nearly everyone around her was part of one single trading clan, cousins and second cousins and third cousins, all with the same auburn hair, green eyes, and freckled skin as the two kids who were always watching Kora. Lafayette wasn't the only stranger among them, but all the other strangers had either paid cash or made some kind of trade for the privilege of company on the road through the grasslands.

She knew they were nearly at the end of that road now. After a month of constant walking, it was only another two days in good weather until she reached the capital city. And then she could leave all these people safely behind.

But two days was starting to feel like two days too many.

Most nights she had gone to the bonfire to trade what she had left of her father's things for a bowl of food, but this night she stayed by the tent with Kora. She could handle a dinner of dry crackers and the last scrapings of her jar of peanut butter.

At least water wasn't in short supply. They had refilled the tanks at a creek the day before.

Although she was starting to worry about Kora's nutritive paste. She had more than enough for two more days. She probably had enough for two more weeks.

But the closer they got to the capital, the more Lafayette worried that whatever her father had made that paste out of, Lafayette might not be able to find it there. Or it might involve some ingredient that would be hard to source. She just didn't know.

She would have help once she got there. Provided she could find her father's old mentor, Uche Okafo. He was a very distinctive-looking man. The tallest man she had ever met, with skin darker even than her mother's, but a cloud of white hair springing fuzzily out of his head in every direction. He wore the finest of clothes, even when arriving at her village after making a journey that must have been just like the one Lafayette was making now with all the cutting grass blades always reaching out for the unwary.

But, unmistakable as he was, he was just one man. And she still couldn't get her mind to grasp the numbers of people who lived in the capital. What would it look like to see a million people all in one place? She couldn't quite picture it without thinking she was making it too big or too small.

Her village had only had about a hundred. And every village she had passed through since leaving home had been about the same size.

The capital was going to be so much bigger. Ten thousand times bigger, in fact. She could do the math. She just couldn't conjure a meaning for that number.

Kora made a whimpering sound and put a paw on Lafayette's knee. Lafayette could feel how badly the dog wanted to say her name, to speak to her like they used to when it was just the two of them. To comfort her.

But Lafayette just scratched all around the dog's ears and said nothing.

Then she packed up everything she had taken out to make her dinner and put it back in the tote, still loaded on the wheelbarrow. She left everything arranged around the spot where she'd put the tent once she collapsed it and folded it up. All she would have to do then was pick up the handles and walk.

Kora followed her into the tiny tent, and if she noticed that Lafayette left her boots on and only laid down on top of her sleeping bag without getting into it, she made no sign of it. She just curled up beside Lafayette, her metal core warm against Lafayette's belly even with the grass matting still covering it.

Neither of them slept. They just laid together in the dark, breathing softly and waiting.

They didn't have to wait long. A rustling sound came outside the walls of the tent. Feet in soft-soled shoes whispering over the jagged remains of cut and burned grass blades. Not quite as soundless as they would be with a few more years of practice, but still very, very quiet.

Then there was another softest of sounds. Lafayette remained perfectly still. But she could imagine a child's little fingers running over the canvas just above her head. Looking for a way to peek inside? And if they didn't find it? Would they just open the front flap?

Before she could find out, another sound hissed out, loud and sibilant. The child's sibling, probably the older one to judge by the chastising tone of that hissing whisper. Lafayette couldn't make out any words—these kids were both really good at keeping things quiet—but she could sense things from the tone of those hisses of air. She heard the younger one sass back then yelp in pain. If there had been a cuffing blow from the elder, Lafayette hadn't heard that at all.

Then the voices went away again. The older one dragging the younger one back to camp? Maybe. Most of the families were just now sitting down to eat food that had required more cooking than Lafayette's cold meal. The younger one had picked the wrong moment to try to sneak away.

Which meant they would be back. When the younger one could break away again, Lafayette knew they would.

With a touch of her hand to Kora's head, she settled in for a long night of wakefulness.

A long night, but not an entire night. No, Lafayette had made her decision.

It was definitely time for her and Kora to go.

CHAPTER 3

With all the tall grass always curving down overhead even around the maintained clearings of the campsites, sunrises and sunsets were not something that Lafayette had seen for herself in days. The sky would lighten, but by the time the sun climbed high enough in the sky to be seen, all the pinks and roses had faded into the hazy whitish blue of midday, and the sun was just an intense disc of blinding light.

Still, Lafayette knew it had been long before sunrise when she and Kora had tiptoed out of camp. If any of the volunteer patrollers keeping watch had seen them go, none of them had said a thing.

Although Lafayette was sure that someone must have seen them. The patrols kept too close of an eye out for bandits. Perhaps, to them and the rest of the caravan, it was good riddance seeing Lafayette and her strange dog leave their company.

Lafayette certainly felt it was good riddance, leaving those staring kids behind.

"I don't think they were bad kids. I just think they thought I was pretty," Kora said all at once, fully out loud. As if continuing some conversation they had already been having.

At least she had let an entire hour go by before she had started talking. Lafayette had to give her that. As much as her mind was half teacher-construct, it was also still half dog. Her impulse control wasn't great.

But Lafayette knew that Kora was constantly alert for signs of bandits. Her ears were on a swivel, and her nose was constantly sampling the various scents that wafted over the road from the grasslands on either side. If she chose now to speak, it was because it was safe to do so.

"If they wanted to pet you, they could've just asked," Lafayette said.

Then she adjusted the grip of her gloved hands on the wheelbarrow handles. It was better than any wheelbarrow she had ever used for chores back in her home village. The wheel didn't hover, but it was attached to a sort of suspension system that let it bounce easily over all the various ruts and potholes without jostling the load and without Lafayette having to do much work directing it beyond keeping it moving forward.

Still, it was a far sight from her father's hover cart, which had needed only a touch to get it moving. No muscle work involved at all.

But Lafayette knew what she was really going to miss now that she and Kora were on their own again was the perimeter fence. They would have to camp when darkness fell, but she had no idea how far along the next campsite was. And even if she did, she couldn't risk sharing it with what would inevitably be the same clan she had just left behind.

She'd have to pitch her tent in the flattest patch of tall grass she could find, out of sight from the road but not too deep into the cutting grass. She'd done it before. She could do it again. But it meant an uncomfortable night on uneven ground.

Which was fine, since she'd want to be awake to keep watch, anyway.

"Just two more days," she said, as much to herself as to Kora. But Kora wagged her tail all the same.

"I can't wait to meet your father's friend," she said conversationally.

"A fellow teacher," Lafayette said.

"Oh, no! It's not remotely the same thing," Kora said. "I was trained to get young children started on their educational paths. An important job, to be sure. But Uche Okafo is a professor at a university."

"And that's different?" Lafayette asked. It was a legitimate question in her mind. She only kind of understood what a university was, beyond meaning just a bigger school building than the one in her village. She wasn't sure if she was grasping the distinction between teacher and professor at all. "I've met Uche Okafo before," she said to Kora. "He wasn't anything like Frank Paine."

"No, Frank Paine was… his own thing," Kora said diplomatically.

Frank Paine had also been a teaching construct, a hologram replica of a real person. Like the construct in Kora, he had been left sleeping for centuries inside the equipment built into the desk of his classroom on board the ship Lafayette's father had found.

Actually, there had been three teachers that Lafayette had interacted with. But while the construct inside Kora—she had asked Lafayette not to call her by her human name of Sameera Adel anymore—had patiently helped Lafayette master first the spoken language of the people of the ship and then the written language, Frank Paine had always treated Lafayette like asking to be taught something was the most annoying thing ever. When he wasn't just looking down his nose at her for simply existing in his space.

Lafayette really hoped that wasn't what "professor" meant. Uche had always seemed so kind when he travelled out to her home village to visit her parents. And even more so when he had come to say goodbye to Lafayette's ailing mother.

But maybe he was different when he was teaching in a classroom. Maybe he was different just when he was home in the capital city. For all she knew, he could be a lot like Frank Paine. She could count on her fingers the number of days she had spent with him.

Maybe this was all a mistake. But she didn't know what else to do, or where else to go. With her mother dead and her father trapped on a ship up in space, she was all on her own. She only knew one person in the whole world who didn't live in the village she had left behind, and that was Uche Okafo.

Lafayette adjusted her grip on the wheelbarrow handles. As if such a gesture could make the nervous twisting of her stomach go away.

"Will you take the journals out tonight? If we're alone?" Kora asked her.

Lafayette wanted to. She longed to turn the pages, to look at all the drawings of plants in her mother's book of medicines, to read over her father's neat, blocky script and try to decipher the schematics he had copied from other, more mysterious sources.

But she didn't dare.

"No, I don't want to unwrap them. Not now, when we're so close," she said.

"That sounds sensible," Kora said. But then she gave Lafayette a little look of sympathy.

Lafayette said nothing, but she knew what that look meant. Kora might not use her human name anymore, but she still remembered her life as a human woman. She had only looked to be about forty, barely older than Lafayette's own parents. But she had had a grandmotherly feeling to her all the same.

Like she would be telling Lafayette what a shame she felt it was for a girl Lafayette's age to have to be sensible at all, if she wasn't sure that her little look had conveyed that all for her without the words being necessary.

"So many maps in your father's journals, and none of them connect to each other," Kora said with a doggy sigh. "Do you think you'll find something in the capital to help you piece them all together?"

"I hope so, but I don't think it's going to be easy," Lafayette said. "My dad spent his whole life looking for the crashed remains of the ships that brought our ancestors here. And in all that time, he only succeeded in finding the one."

"He can probably access all the systems on the ship now, including the records of the last days," Kora said. "He might already know where the other four ships are, or have a good idea where to start looking."

"Maybe," Lafayette said as noncommittally as she could.

It was almost worse, the thought that her father had unlocked all the secrets on his own. He had no way of communicating with her or anyone else on the surface, let alone getting down himself.

And all he had for company were the other two constructs. Assuming, if he tired of Frank Paine's brand of company, he could figure out how to turn the middle teacher on. Yusuf Khan was more like Sameera, patient and kind. He seemed like he would be pleasant company. Lafayette had been expecting to work more with him to advance her own education.

But that was before she'd realized that if she didn't help Frank Paine launch the ship, it was going to explode. And as much as it tore at her heart knowing that her father was still trapped in space, it was still better than being exploded inside of that crater.

"Do you know what I'm most worried about?" Lafayette found herself saying.

"That I'll run out of that nutritive paste you feed me?" Kora asked in an almost cheery voice.

"What?" Lafayette all but stammered. That wasn't what she had been about to say at all. In fact, she hadn't thought Kora even knew they were running low on that.

"I see your face after you give me my evening's portion," Kora said. "You look at how much is left, and I can see you doing the math over again every single time."

"We have enough to get to the city for sure," Lafayette assured her.

"Then Uche Okafo will help you get more," Kora said.

Lafayette said nothing. She certainly hoped that was true. But when Uche had asked Lafayette to come back to the capital city with him, Kora hadn't been a robot dog yet. She had just been an old, graying dog who never left Lafayette's mother's side.

Because, when Uche had made that offer, Lafayette's mother hadn't even been dead yet.

A lot had changed since then. Lafayette was sure his offer for a place to stay was still good. The timing had been bad, but that wasn't his fault. He had made it to her when he did because he hadn't had any choice in the matter. He had seen Lafayette's mother was dying, and he knew that her father was far away, all but unreachable.

But Uche hadn't been able to stay in the village any longer, not even to be there when his former student finally passed from the disease no one recognized, let alone could cure. And obviously Lafayette hadn't been able to leave with him when he'd gone back to the capital. Not with her mother still lingering on in her sickbed.

He had told her to come find him whenever she needed him. And she knew he had meant it.

She was just less sure if his offer of a home also extended to complications like Kora.

And offering Lafayette a place to stay was quite a different thing from offering to help Lafayette in continuing her father's very dangerous life mission.

Or to help in the all but impossible task of trying to rescue him from orbit.

Lafayette swallowed hard, then forced her brain to go back to the problem of imagining what a million people all living in one place must look like. It was an effective distraction from her other fears. The anxiety of how overwhelming it was all going to be was easier to manage than her other anxieties.

Kora's ears both switched forward at once, and she hunched down low. Lafayette was sure the hair on the dog's back would be bristling up into a ridge if she still had any there.

Lafayette quickly looked around, then found a gap between two monstrous tufts of grass. She drove the wheelbarrow into it. The roots of the grasses tore up the ground even worse than the ruts in the road did, and she actually had to lean in hard to keep the wheel bouncing over them.

She didn't get far out of sight before she heard feet pounding the hard pack of the dirt road, but it would have to be enough. She directed Kora to hide behind one of the grass tufts, slicing the sleeve of her shirt on an exposed blade in the process. She only grazed her skin, but she regretted the damage to her shirt. She was quickly running out of clothes, almost as quickly as she was running out of food.

Then the pounding drew closer, and she saw the outline of a single woman with a tall pack on her shoulders running down the center of the road. The top of her pack had a parasol jammed into it, tilted forward to protect the runner's head from the sun. Lafayette fought the urge to wipe the sweat from her brow with the mangled remains of her shirtsleeve and wished she had a parasol of her own.

It looked like a really good idea, particularly if running all day was how this woman was getting from place to place.

The woman's dark skin and honey-colored hair marked her as definitely not part of the caravan that Lafayette and Kora had left behind. And she didn't look like a trader. What could she fit inside a single rucksack that was worth traveling to sell?

She didn't look like a law enforcement patrol either, although Lafayette had only ever seen those from a distance. They usually traveled in groups of five, but never less than two. And this woman was alone.

She had to be some kind of messenger. Running to deliver some missive. But the messengers that had come to Lafayette's hometown had always traveled in pairs for safety.

Was it safer here, for this woman to be running alone? Or was her mission just that urgent?

She was jogging at a very brisk pace. And while she was alert, she didn't seem particularly concerned. Her darting glances missed Lafayette and Kora entirely. She wasn't being anywhere near as watchful as the patrols that protected the caravan.

Then, as quickly as she appeared, the woman was out of sight past the next bend in the road. Lafayette still stood in the shadows for as long as she could handle the clouds of mosquitos eagerly feeding off her blood.

It was like they had been waiting their entire lives for someone like her to blunder into their territory and weren't going to miss the opportunity for a feast.

At last, she pushed the wheelbarrow back up onto the road, and she and Kora resumed their walk.

One more day after this one. They only had to keep this up for one more day.

And surely the closer they got to the capital city, the less likely they were to encounter bandits in the grass. That woman on her own hadn't looked worried. All of her attention had been on maintaining her fast jog.

She hadn't seen Lafayette and Kora in the grass. Or she had, and she hadn't found either of them particularly remarkable. Lafayette thought it was the former, but the idea of the latter wouldn't quite leave her.

It would be so nice, not to be particularly remarkable.

CHAPTER 4

Lafayette didn't realize just how close to civilization she and Kora were when they stopped to camp on the first night. Not until she knew it had to be long after sunset, but the sky was still faintly luminous. Like it was never going to get dark here.

And more so to the east, which wasn't normal. But then again, the color of that light was nothing like the rosy glow from the setting sun. It wasn't firelight either. It was more like the light she remembered from inside the ship after her father accidentally turned on the power. Not so bright, not so intense. But the diffuse, seemingly sourceless light glowed all night long.

They spent a restless night, both of them stiffening in alertness at every rustle of noise. But, aside from the constantly droning insects and the minor skittering of little animals creeping through the roots of grass, there was nothing to be alarmed about. Nothing came close to their tent, anyway.

But the brightness of that sky intrigued Lafayette so much she crawled back out of the tent several times just to look up at it. She still couldn't see the source, not with the tall grass all around her. But the light was blue, pink, and soft white, especially where it reflected off of the low-hanging clouds. That was more variety than the lights she had seen on the ship.

And it was so bright, she could barely make out the dot of light that was her father on the ship as it crossed the sky in its inescapable orbit.

Breakfast was the last of the crackers along with a tiny bag of dried berries she couldn't even remember acquiring. She had found the crushed paper bag lurking under the folded clothes she had been saving for once her journey was through, although it was still too soon to put them on now. After that little bit of food was gone, she packed up the tent and took up the handles of her wheelbarrow.

Then, not five minutes later, she and Kora were walking into a town. Although she didn't think this was where the light had been coming from. It was both too close to where she had been sleeping, but also too small.

It definitely wasn't big enough to fit a million people. Not even close. It was a little larger than her hometown, but where the huts of her village had been almost randomly arranged along the banks of the winding creek and around the massive trunk of their central tree, the houses here were lined up in neat rows.

They had walls around them that partitioned a section of land around each house, which felt off-putting to Lafayette. She was used to a more open design of village living.

But all the fences had gates, and those gates all stood open to offer views of the yards and front stoops beyond. Most of the stoops had people on them, parents watching children playing in the yards while tinkering with something in their hands. She didn't see anyone weaving cloth or baskets or spinning yarn, though, the sorts of activities she was used to seeing back home. Here, everyone seemed to be building something delicate out of bits of metal.

Rather like her father had always been doing his entire life. Even the tools they were using looked familiar to her from watching her father work. Apparently, that sort of tinkering wasn't as odd as she always assumed it was. But she had never seen anyone but her father do it before this very morning.

No one seemed to mind Lafayette looking in on them. If she

happened to catch anyone's eye, they would smile or raise a hand in greeting. They didn't stop their work for more than a moment, but even that much personal contact was treating her with more friendliness than she was used to getting from people who surely saw her as a stranger.

Or, frankly, even as a neighbor, like back in her old village. Her mother, as the resident healer, had filled a necessary niche. But Lafayette had been something that had to be tolerated to keep that healer close.

No one had been cruel to her. But no one had ever let her forget she was something extra, part of the cost of having access to her mother.

The road took a turn on the far end of the little town and carried on through another patch of the tall grasslands, but this was less dense than what she had been traveling through for days. There were gaps between the bunches, and the ground between looked rich and dark. She saw debris here and there, like the charred remains of burned grass from the clearing of the campsites.

This area was some weird combination of wild and maintained that she couldn't quite grasp the point of. But it was interesting. And she wouldn't complain about the extra breeze it let through.

The road dipped down a gentle hill, then started a slow but steady climb. But to where she couldn't tell. The grass was still just too tall.

But then two more roads appeared on either side of the road they were walking on, sloping in from the grasslands to join with hers and make a single, wider road.

Which was also a busier road. There were lots of people walking with her now, some with handcarts or wheelbarrows like hers. The road was still climbing uphill, but the run of it was straight now, and she could see for quite a way ahead. A caravan of wagons was taking their time off on the righthand side of the road, but not the caravan she had left behind. A different group with darker hair and browner skin, although still likely cousins to judge by the repeating facial features they shared.

Kora was drawing looks now, but not the kind that worried Lafayette. The kids who saw her now would run over to ask if they could pet her, which Lafayette allowed, so long as they could do it without slowing her and Kora down.

For her part, Kora seemed to thrive on the attention. Her trotting step was even more prancing than usual, and her tail never slowed its happy swishing back and forth.

They passed through another town of walled-in houses, just a little larger than the first. And then, just after midday, another. This one had a large common area in the center of all those houses, with shady trees and people selling hot, fresh food off of carts.

Lafayette debated trading the tent or the wheelbarrow for some skewers of meat, but opted not to. She didn't know for sure she wasn't going to need them again. She only hoped she didn't.

And hope wasn't enough for her to be willing to make such a sacrifice. So she ignored the growling of her belly and tried to pick up her pace.

The towns were almost continuous now, with the grasslands between little more than dividing strips. Lafayette listened to the voices chatting all around her, relieved to find she understood every word. And she was confident when she repeated phrases under her breath that her accent was very close to correct.

She had been worried about that. She had only ever heard the capital city dialect on those few short times when Uche Okafo had been visiting. Then she had learned the far older but still related dialect that the ship constructs all spoke. Her fear that the longer exposure to the dead version of their common language would ruin what little skill she had with the current local version faded from her mind.

Leaving just all her other fears. So many fears.

The slope of the road grew steeper, so gradually she was at first not even sure if she was just imagining it. After a long day of walking, feeling like each step was harder than the last was usually how things went.

But then they finally reached the crest of the hill. The caravan that had been hugging the side of the road was now blocking the entire width of it, as the line of wagons wound their way around a single broken-down wagon whose sputtering engine was putting clouds of ashy black smoke into the air but completely failing to turn the axle.

So Lafayette set her wheelbarrow down to wait for the traffic to clear. Rubbing her sore hands, she spared a glance back the way they'd come. The road behind them ran almost due west, straight towards the horizon, and she was hoping for a glimpse of the setting sun for the first time in days.

And she did indeed see the sun setting almost directly over the path behind her.

But she could also see over the tops of the grasses from where she was standing. And as numerous as the towns she had walked through had seemed, she had only passed through a fraction of them. They were everywhere, like dots of rain on a flat surface that spread out to almost touch each other. There was really very little grassland left between them.

Was this what a million people looked like?

Then she turned to look east again. The broken-down wagon had finally moved, as had all the others, and the way ahead was clear. So Lafayette picked up the wheelbarrow handles and walked the rest of the way to the very top of the hill.

And saw the city spread out below her. The road ran only a little further on, stopping at an enormous gate built into an even more enormous stone wall. And that wall ran in a ring far to the north and to the south, enclosing a place that was even more densely built and filled with light than the towns in the grasslands behind her had been.

There was so much to see, even at this distance. Buildings stacked on top of buildings, taller on the sides then dipping down in the center of the walled ring, as if the entire city were one large bowl. She was too far away to see any details. She couldn't make out any roads, so she guessed the buildings were both tall and set very close to each other. Here and there stood a single taller tower, each with squared-off sides but a domed top. She could just make out sloping lines connecting one tower to the next, always in pairs.

She puzzled over that for a moment, until she saw something vaguely wagon-shaped moving slowly along one pair of those lines, heading towards the arched opening under the dome of one of those towers.

And then, with a suddenness that had her gasping out loud, she realized what she was looking at. Her father had described them to her once, when he had been telling her about the city.

They were trams. That was the way most people moved around the city. The streets were too narrow and winding for wagons on the ground to be of much use. It would take forever to get from one place to another that way.

The trams glided over everything.

But those towers were not the tallest part of the city. Nor was the stone wall that contained the entire place.

No, the tallest part was at the very heart of the city. A single structure jutted far up into the sky, topped by what looked like another miniature version of the same city. But while that mini-city was the same beige and brown tones of stone as the buildings and walls of the city below, the structure it stood on top of was something else entirely.

It was impossible to see clearly, as the light of the setting sun behind Lafayette was striking it with all of its rosiest-colored sunbeams. And there were a lot of structures built on the sides of that spire, not as impressive as the mini-city on top, but of the same stone colors.

And yet, something was different about the spire itself. From the way it was reflecting that light, Lafayette knew it had to be metal. No one could build something so thin and tall out of stone. It was impossible.

No, it was definitely metal. Metal, which everywhere else was so rare. Only small tools were made of metal. Kora had more metal in her than Lafayette had ever seen in one place before leaving her village. The bits and pieces her father recovered in his archaeology work had been useful for her to sell specifically because metal was so rare.

But here, they built an entire tower of it. Just to hold up another little city.

But she set her wonder at that sight aside to scan the skies for signs of anything floating up there. Because her favorite drawings in her father's books when she was a little kid had been of the dirigibles and balloons that filled the skies of the capital city in his oldest books. But there was no sign of them now. Perhaps it was the wrong time of day. She'd look again tomorrow.

Still, this was it. This glittering vision of human activity. This was the place she had walked for days to reach.

Her parents' past. But hopefully, Lafayette's future.

Lafayette leaned in on the wheelbarrow and got it rolling down the hill, towards that gate and everything that laid beyond it.

CHAPTER 5

Lafayette and Kora passed through the open doors of the gate in a crowd of other people. But on the far side of that gate, the crowd immediately broke apart. Mostly because it had no choice. There was no more wide road, just a bunch of narrow, twisty roads that forked off in every possible direction. They were all paved, but the stones they were paved with were uneven in most places and outright missing in others.

These streets reminded Lafayette of runnels in dried mud left behind after all the water had run away. They were deep but meandering.

And she had no idea which one she should take.

Kora was looking up at her with those questioning dark brown eyes, but Lafayette just gave her a reassuring smile before looking around for any kind of clue.

Uche Okafo was a professor at a university. And a university was bigger than a school. She had those facts to work with, anyway.

If a university was big, it was likely someone could point her in the right direction.

She looked around for a friendly pair of eyes. But mostly what she noticed straight away was a number of kids watching her. They were scattered all around her. One was up on a balcony looking down at the stream of people coming out of the gate from that vantage point. Another was weaving through the crowd, slinking through without ever jostling anyone or ever losing sight of Lafayette.

Another was in a darker space too narrow to be a street, little more than a gap between the city wall and the first of the buildings.

They were all staring at her. Her, not Kora.

As she noticed these kids, they all stared openly at her as if silently announcing their presence.

And then they just… melted away. Disappeared in the blink of an eye.

And yet, Lafayette still felt those eyes on her. Invisible to her. But she was all too visible to them.

Then a smell of roasting meat washed over her, even as she heard the hiss of steam escaping. She turned to see a food cart just behind her, tucked down one of those anonymous streets. The woman standing over that cart sprayed some sort of dark brown liquid over that meat and the fire hissed even louder than before, erupting high into the air to lick at the flanks of that juicy meat.

Lafayette looked down at what she had left in the wheelbarrow, but there wasn't much. Her one good set of clothes. Her couple of sets of road-battered clothes. The tent and the wheelbarrow itself.

But she still wasn't ready to give those up.

Then she nudged the lid off of one of the crates, the one that held her cooking utensils. They didn't do her much good now that she had no food left to cook.

She edged her wheelbarrow closer to the food cart just as the woman was replacing the dome-like lid over the cooking meat.

"Hungry?" she asked Lafayette with a friendly smile as she saw the girl and the dog drawing closer to her.

"I don't have any money," Lafayette said. "But would you take something in trade?"

The woman's eyes swept over her, taking in every bit of mud that clung to her boots, the rips and stains from the grass blades on her shirt and pants, the dirt that Lafayette was all too aware was clinging to every inch of her sweaty skin. She fought the urge to brush the dust from her red-tipped buns of hair. She would only create a cloud close to that woman's food, covered or not.

"You've been walking far," the woman said. It wasn't quite a question.

"Yes," Lafayette admitted.

"On your own," the woman went on.

"With my dog, Kora," Lafayette said.

At the sound of her name, Kora sat politely, her tail swishing a clean patch on the paving stones behind her.

The woman made a noncommittal sound at that. But then she peered at the contents of Lafayette's wheelbarrow.

"What were you looking to trade?" she asked.

"I have cooking tools, if that's useful to you," Lafayette said, taking the lid off of the tote and gesturing for the woman to peer inside.

"Good quality, if a little roughly kept," the woman said.

Lafayette felt her cheeks flush hotly with embarrassment at that assessment, but said nothing.

"Don't have much use for a stewpot, although that looks to be the cleanest thing here," the woman said, almost as if musing to herself.

Then she reached in and pulled out a long-handled metal fork and spoon. They were a set, the handle of one sliding into a mechanism on the other so that they locked together. Handy when cooking with fire, and easy to keep neatly organized when packing and unpacking while traveling.

"Can you part with this?" the woman asked. She peered up at Lafayette with a single intense eye, the other lost in the shadows of her loose waves of hair.

"I can," Lafayette said. "I'm done traveling, now that I'm here."

"Are you?" the woman said, almost as if she didn't quite believe it.

Then she turned her attention back to the fork and spoon, turning them over in her hands as if examining them for possible defects. Lafayette's stomach growling loudly was the only sound between them, and few of the people coming through the gate were passing down this particular road.

But the light was intense, throwing everything it wasn't touching into sharp shadows. Like that woman's other eye.

Not light from the sun, Lafayette realized, and looked up to see they were standing under a large globe of light. The quality of the light itself was like what she had seen on the ship, but the fixture it was emitting from was quite different. It looked like a rectangular box that had been roughly crafted in a forge from iron, the sides an even rougher version of glass.

"I'll take them," the woman said at last, and Lafayette looked back down from the light. She saw nothing but spots in front of her eyes for a few seconds. But she could smell the meat smell grow stronger again as the steam dripping from the inside of the lid met the flame with another chorus of hisses.

And then she felt the woman shoving something into her hand. Or rather, three somethings. Three skewers of meat.

"Thank you," Lafayette said, insanely grateful but trying hard not to sound like she had expected to get far less in return. She didn't want to seem like she didn't know how things worked here in the city.

Although she absolutely didn't know how things worked.

"Do you know where you're going from here?" the woman asked. The sharpness of her tone had not abated at all, but Lafayette had stopped flinching away from it. It was a wonder what a little warm food in her belly did for her mental state.

"I'm looking for a professor. At the university," Lafayette said.

She knew she was pronouncing those words in the city dialect just a shade too carefully. But she hoped, since she was speaking them around a mouthful of meat, maybe the woman wouldn't notice.

But that one visible eye was still peering at her intently, and the woman let another long, awkward silence stretch between them. Lafayette was just starting to fear the woman was going to call her out as a liar or something when the woman suddenly jabbed a finger off towards a direction behind Lafayette. North and east from where they were standing.

"Follow that road there, no matter how much it tries to turn away beneath you," she said. "It's a bit of a walk from here to the campus, and I wager you don't have a pass for the tramways. But if you just stay on that road, you can't miss it. You'll see the students before you even see the buildings. They're hard to miss."

"Thank you," Lafayette said, trying to make quick work of the third skewer so she could pick up the wheelbarrow handles again. The first two she had bolted down in a flash, but she was actually feeling a little full now.

It was a lot of meat. But whatever was in that brown liquid the woman basted it with was quite possibly the best thing Lafayette had ever tasted.

And on the ship with her father, she had even had bacon.

"The lights stay on all night?" Lafayette asked, again around a mouthful of meat. She tried not to imagine what her mother would say.

"Yeah, but this is a part of town you'll still want to get out of as quickly as you can," the woman told her. "They close the gates in another hour, and after that, it isn't safe here for anyone."

"Don't you live here?" Lafayette asked.

"I have my ways," the woman said with a little wave of her hand. "But you obviously are not prepared for anything. I would walk with you, if it weren't such a long way. Move briskly, and keep your wits about you."

"Like the bandits on the road," Lafayette said as she handed the now-empty skewers back to the woman.

"Maybe," the woman said as she took the metal implements from Lafayette and dropped them into a bin of soapy water in the bottom part of her cart.

Lafayette heard that "maybe" as more of a "bandits would be preferable," but decided not to press.

"Thank you," she said instead, and leaned over the wheelbarrow handles to get the whole thing moving. Light as it had become, it bounced easily even over the rough surface of the road.

The woman just pointed out the road again in case Lafayette had forgotten. And she kept pointing at it until Lafayette made the first turning and the two of them lost sight of each other.

She could hear voices all around her, and there were globes of light hanging over every place where her road crossed another.

The crossings were crazy. Her road almost never met another that was completely perpendicular. Most were at steep angles, and the buildings around those crossings were built into wedge shapes to fill that space.

Or the wedge-shaped buildings were why the roads were so crazy, Lafayette couldn't really tell cause from effect.

But the further she got from the gate, the quieter the voices around her became. Now they were all indoors, behind closed shutters, just barely audible. She occasionally passed another person or two walking on the street. None of them more than glanced at her in a way that wasn't exactly friendly, but was far from hostile.

And the feeling of being watched had largely passed, although Lafayette was constantly alert for its return. She didn't like that feeling, of being watched by someone she couldn't see.

Once, she heard a grinding sound and looked up to see the bottom of a tram rolling overhead, crossing her road towards some unseen tower off to her left. It really was like a caravan wagon, if much larger. And with the wheels on top, rolling over the tops of those heavy cables.

Sunset was long past, but being down in the glow of all those artificial lights made the stars in the sky impossible to see. Lafayette couldn't even catch a glimpse of either of the moons. It was impossible for her to guess at the time now.

But just when she had convinced herself that in all the quiet stillness it was surely the very middle of the night, she started to hear voices again. Young voices, laughing and talking over each other.

Then the road she was on just ended. All that stood in front of her was a large square of grass. But not the grass that grew in cutting blades high up to the sky. No, this was soft, delicate grass. And it could barely grow at all, from the looks of it. It was constantly being squashed flat under the passage of so many feet.

Lafayette kept heading in a straight line in case the road she was meant to be following continued on from the far side of the open square. But the woman's words echoed in her mind, about not letting the road try to turn away beneath her.

Had that just happened? Was she lost?

Then a group of six people about her age passed in front of her. Unlike the caravan people, they didn't look enough alike to all be cousins. And yet they were all wearing the same thing, basically. Dark blue pants with a matching jacket over a lighter blue blousy tunic.

And they were carrying books. That was what really tipped it off for Lafayette.

Books. *Books.* The things her parents always had to hide away from the eyes of others. And these kids were just carrying them around as if they were nothing at all.

Students. They had to be students.

She had done it. She had found the university.

Now she just had to find Uche Okafo.

CHAPTER 6

Lafayette had no idea how to start searching for a man she hadn't seen in months while standing in an open square in the middle of the night, the buildings around her strange and mysterious with all of their dark windows staring blankly down at her.

So she did the one thing that had yet to fail her this entire journey.

She picked the six people in sight who clearly knew where they were going and turned her wheelbarrow until she was following them.

Kora made a questioning whimper sort of sound, as close as she dared come to not sounding like a dog.

"They're going somewhere, right?" Lafayette whispered down to her as they walked. "Somewhere where there will be other people. Maybe people who know where to find Uche Okafo."

Kora didn't make any noise in reply. But Lafayette was getting a skeptical vibe from her.

Then, for no reason that Lafayette could see, one of the girls in the group she was following broke into a laughing run. One of the boys tore after her, and then all six were running.

Which wasn't something Lafayette was going to try to do with the wheelbarrow. She could probably manage it. The grass was easier to move over than the roads, with all the ground here worn smooth and even.

But there was no subtle way to do it. And she still wasn't eager to draw more attention than she had to.

Then a door off to her left shut with a slam, and Lafayette peered up into the darkness of an overhanging front entryway on top of a flight of six stone steps. The whole edifice was built ridiculously huge. An entire class of kids could sit on those steps, using them like an auditorium. And the space under that overhang was so tall the door itself had to be twice the size of a standard door.

There was a shuffling sound, footsteps over stone, and then a girl emerged into the patches of light that criss-crossed the steps without penetrating the space closer to the door.

Like the other students, she was only a little older than Lafayette's age of eighteen. She had a short cap of auburn hair that swung in a sheet on the right side of her face as she bent her head to look at the stack of books in her arms as she skipped down the steps. The light danced over her hair, pulling out darker and lighter highlights in an almost hypnotic pattern.

Then the girl reached the bottom of the steps and looked up at Lafayette as if startled to find her there. Which, given that Lafayette was very much not wearing a blue outfit and was, in fact, standing there with the handles of a battered wheelbarrow in her hands, was entirely fair.

Still, the girl gave her a nervous smile, sweeping that wave of hair back behind her ear before pinning Lafayette down with eyes as green as jade.

"I hope you didn't need the library," she said with an apologetic wince. "We just closed for the night, and tomorrow is the school holiday. We don't open again until the day after."

"No, I didn't need the library," Lafayette said. Although she wasn't sure why this girl would've jumped to that conclusion. Granted, there *were* a number of books hidden inside her wheelbarrow. But this girl couldn't possibly know that.

Still, a library was a place to find information. She knew that from her parents' stories. Maybe she *did* need a library.

"Do you work here?" Lafayette asked.

The girl looked down at a key in her hand and tucked it away inside a pocket before nodding. "It's a work study."

Which meant nothing to Lafayette, but if she stopped to follow up on every question that burst into her mind begging to be asked, she'd be out here all night.

"I'm trying to find someone who lives here at the university," Lafayette said. "Maybe you can help me?"

The girl had just noticed Kora sitting by Lafayette's ankle and was smiling down at the dog. Kora's tail was brushing the ground behind her clean again. Neither of them seemed to realize that Lafayette had just spoken.

Then the girl turned her attention back to Lafayette. "There are a ton of students here. I know a lot of them, but just a small fraction of the total number, really. You would probably have to ask the help desk in the administrative building. But they're also closed."

She made another apologetic little flinch of her face before bringing her smile back up to full brightness.

"It's not a student, actually. It's a professor," Lafayette said.

"Well, that narrows it down a bit," the girl said with confident optimism.

"A former teacher," Lafayette added, hoping that change didn't make things harder again.

"Still leaving on campus?" the girl asked.

"I believe so," Lafayette said.

"Then I'm sure I know them," the girl said, stepping closer to Lafayette, a little further out from the glow of the light. "I help coordinate their housing and personal needs."

"In addition to working in the library," Lafayette said.

The girl laughed but blushed. "I like to be helpful," she said. "I'm Margo, by the way. Margo Weiss."

"Lafayette Eloi," Lafayette said.

"And this is?" Margo said, smiling down at Kora again.

"This is my dog, Kora," Lafayette said.

Kora made a happy bark at the sound of her name. A very convincingly canine sort of bark. Kora was getting better at pretending to be an ordinary dog.

"And the professor you're looking for?" Margo asked.

"Uche Okafo," Lafayette said. "He used to teach—"

"I know him," Margo said, cutting off Lafayette's words in a way that felt not just deliberate but somehow urgent.

Lafayette frowned at her in confusion, but Margo just smiled at her again. Although the edges of that smile looked worried somehow.

Like maybe Margo was feeling what Lafayette had felt before. Like they were being watched by people they couldn't see.

Lafayette started to look around, to see if she could spot anyone lurking in the shadows. But Margo lunged towards her, catching her arm as if desperate to drag Lafayette's attention back to herself.

"I can walk you there," Margo said. "It's not even out of my way, since it lets me mark as done my weekly check-in with him."

"OK," Lafayette said in a slow drawl. She didn't understand most of that. Except for the part about walking her to Uche Okafo.

But that was the only part that really mattered.

"It's just this way," Margo said, indicating a road off to their left with a tip of her head that sent that sleek wave of hair swinging again.

They walked in silence for several minutes, until the library and the plaza were a couple of blocks behind them. Then it was like all the tension left Margo's body at once. Her grip on her books loosened, and her tight stride became more of a stroll than an urgent march. She gave Lafayette a shy smile. "Okay, we can talk here. Tell me, how do you know Professor Okafo?"

"He taught my parents," Lafayette said. But she couldn't help throwing a glance back over her shoulder. The library was well out of sight now. But had someone been there watching them? Was Margo right that they were safe now?

"Really! How interesting," Margo said. Lafayette looked at Margo's face as closely as she could as they walked through alternating patches of light and shadow. They were on a paved road once more, but wider and smoother than the road she had followed before.

She didn't think that Margo was faking her enthusiasm. But Lafayette in her entire life had never met anyone who found anything she said interesting. With the possible exception of Kora, and to a lesser extent, her parents.

Then Margo sucked in a breath, a sound like something had just clicked in her brain. "He just got back from a long trip to some village far to the south of here. Did that have something to do with you?"

"Yeah," Lafayette admitted. "He came to see my mother before she passed."

"Oh, I'm so sorry," Margo said, shifting her books to one arm so she could reach out with the other and squeeze Lafayette's shoulder.

The sudden, kind gesture was startling. And it was tempting to stop walking and just soak in the casual sympathy of that touch. Especially when Margo didn't draw her hand back. She just gave Lafayette's shoulder a few comforting rubs.

"That's why I'm here now," Lafayette said when she could trust her voice not to warble on her. "Uche wanted me to come back here with him, but he couldn't wait for my mother's illness to run its course. So he came back without me, and I waited until it was all over. And now I'm here."

"Yes," Margo said softly, and withdrew her hand to tuck that hair back behind her ear again. It slipped forward again almost at once, but she didn't seem to notice. She just moved a little closer to Lafayette and said in the softest of voices, "He wasn't supposed to go at all. He's being watched now more closely than ever. I'll get you there safely, I promise you. You don't need to worry about me making trouble for you. I like to be helpful, remember?"

"Sure," Lafayette said. Then felt compelled to add a quick, "Thanks."

And tried to hide her rising panic as she shoved down the urge to ask so many more questions.

But she had a feeling she knew the drill here. It was just like when Uche used to meet her parents in their village. Certain discussions were only had in the dead of night, with all the doors shut and the windows shuttered.

Discussions carried on in whispers. In the oldest version of the capital city dialect, the one that was almost like the dead version that the constructs on the ship had spoken.

"You'll be safe," Margo said again. "You'll see. I didn't mean to make you nervous."

"No, I understand," Lafayette said. Although she didn't understand much at all. Only that she knew Margo was being completely, honestly sincere with her. She wasn't faking her anxious concern.

"It's just that he was a history professor, you know?" Margo said. Her whisper now was so low it was almost inaudible over the hiss of the wheelbarrow's wheel over the paved road.

And Lafayette supposed that did explain everything, or at least enough. Her father had been an archaeologist, hunting for clues to where their people's ancestors had come from. And she had known that was not spoken of aloud. Not safely.

She had known that even before her father had truly warned her. He had spelled it all out. In a great hurry, as their time together was cut so short, so fast by the ship's engine about to either take off or explode. It had been most of their goodbye to each other, that warning.

That they weren't the only ones who knew about the ship in the crater, and the four other scattered somewhere over the planet. That they were just the only ones who knew but weren't *supposed* to know.

That if Central Planning knew she knew, they would stop her from telling others. Even if they only suspected she knew, they would hurt her to keep her silent.

That she should trust no one save Uche Okafo.

"Are you all right?" Margo asked, breaking into Lafayette's painful reliving of that last moment with her dad before he'd been taken so far from her.

Which Lafayette was grateful for. She had relived that moment enough. And going through it all again never changed the outcome.

"Yes, thanks," Lafayette said, and tried for a smile of her own. It didn't remotely match Margo's bright, friendly smile. She doubted it even touched her eyes much. But even that small turn-up of the corners of her mouth brought an answering smile from Margo. And that kind of did make her feel better.

"It's up this way, behind the cafeteria building," Margo said, pointing up a steep, deeply rutted lane that ran between two buildings to a second, higher road.

Lafayette tried not to sigh as she leaned in for one last push of the wheelbarrow. But she was so very tired.

Then suddenly it was lighter, as Margo shifted her books to her other arm once more to help Lafayette push. She could only spare one hand, but it was enough. The wheelbarrow really was lighter than before. And the wheel's suspension responded to any kind of push at all.

The higher road was without any of the globes of light that Lafayette had started to accept as a given all over the city. But Margo didn't seem to need one to guide her. She kept her hand on the wheelbarrow, helping Lafayette steer through the shadows until they reached an even darker side alley between two buildings.

Lafayette didn't even see the low, narrow door set in the side of the building on the left of that alley. But she heard Margo's bright, confident knock.

And wished she felt half as brightly confident herself. But her heart was beating in the middle of her throat, all but choking her with its nervous pounding.

The door would open. The door would open and, one way or another, Lafayette's entire life was about to change.

She had gotten this far with the hope that this change would be for the better. But now that her journey had ended here, in a dark alley off a dark street, knocking at the crudest wooden door she had ever seen, the last of that hope was dying away. Like the last guttering of a candle.

Quick, she willed inside her own mind. Quick, open the door before it's gone.

But she couldn't have said if she was directing those thoughts at herself, Margo, Uche Okafo, or the entire universe.

She just kept thinking them.

Quick.

Quick.

Please.

The door opened.

CHAPTER 7

At first, Lafayette didn't recognize the man standing in the doorway. The only light was coming from directly behind him, and the stooped figure she was seeing in silhouette was nothing like the man she had seen just two months before.

But the light passing through the fuzzy cloud of hair around his head was familiar.

Margo showed no hesitation. The minute the door was open, she stepped closer into the light with both hands extended to take his. "Professor Okafo. I hope you're doing well. I found a friend of yours wandering in the plaza in front of the library, and so I've brought her to you."

"A friend?" Uche repeated in a wavering voice.

Lafayette swallowed hard and stepped closer, so that the light from the doorway fell on her face. Uche's was still in shadow, but she could no longer deny it was him.

It was him, but he was so much changed since she'd seen him last. Like he'd aged a decade in just a couple of months.

"Uche," she said nervously. As much as it didn't feel like the polite way to start this conversation, she couldn't stop herself from asking, "Did visiting my mother make you ill?"

"Oh, no, dear," he said, pulling his hands free of Margo's to clasp Lafayette's in turn. There was a tremor to his hands, but his grip when he squeezed her hands was as strong and warm as ever. "No, what was eating away at her was not contagious."

"I don't know where your village is, but for as long as the professor was away, it must've been quite a journey," Margo said.

Lafayette decided if Margo was fishing for the name of her village, she wasn't going to give it. "It was a long way," was all she said, and that after the silence stretched on too long and too awkward for her to continue just saying nothing.

"And now you've come the whole way yourself," Uche said, gently tugging on Lafayette's hands to draw her into the house.

"I should get my things from the wheelbarrow first," Lafayette said, taking half a step back.

Then Kora made an inquiring sort of bark. Lafayette, after weeks of traveling without Kora having the full use of her voice, was getting pretty good at guessing the feeling behind the sounds of her dog's voice.

She guessed that the doggy part of Kora wasn't sure if she recognized Uche or not, and the construct part wasn't sure what to do about the doggy part's nervousness.

"Hello, Kora," Uche said, using the doorframe to lower down to one knee and hold out a hand for the dog to sniff. "I'm sure I smell different from what you're used to, but it's still me."

Kora snuffled all over the outstretched hand, then seemed to catch one scent in particular that chased all her skittishness away. She gave a happy bark and pawed at Uche, tail wagging like mad.

When this reunion was done, Uche waved away Margo and Lafayette's attempts to help and again used the doorframe to get back on his feet. He looked from Lafayette to Margo and back again, but seemed to be unable to find the words to say anything.

Lafayette felt a nervous tickle run up her spine. Uche didn't trust Margo. That was clear. And he had, in fact, told her specifically to trust no one but him. She could see he was waiting for Margo to go before saying any but the blandest of things to Lafayette.

But had Lafayette already said too much? She hadn't named her hometown, although she wasn't sure if that even mattered. She definitely hadn't said anything she knew was secret.

But there were so many things she didn't know about what was and wasn't secret. Best to keep holding her tongue.

"Well, I should leave you two to catch up," Margo said, adjusting the books in her arms in a way that said those arms were getting tired from the carrying of them. "I'll check in with you later this week to see how you're doing, all right, Professor? I can bring you some more of my grandmother's ginger tea with turmeric that you like so much. I still have a batch left from the last package she sent me."

"That would be lovely, dear," Uche said.

"It was nice meeting you, Lafayette Eloi," Margo said. "If you're planning to stay with Uche, I'm sure we'll be seeing more of each other, too. If you like, once you've settled in a little, I can give you a little tour of the area? Introduce you to some of my friends?"

"Oh, yes," Lafayette said, but her attempts at a smile of gratitude were not quite successful. Her initial reaction to the invitation was an enthusiastic yes. And yet, although the same benign smile never left his face, Lafayette sensed a subtle warning in Uche's body language.

Don't trust anyone. Right.

Still, she kind of hoped that Margo just wrote Lafayette's weird response off as her being tired from her long journey. Which was also true.

But Margo just gave them both a wave and disappeared into the shadows back the way they'd come.

"We should get inside," Uche said, all traces of benign politeness gone, replaced with a cautious sort of urgency. He gestured for Lafayette to get in so he could shut the door.

But she couldn't just yet. "My father's things are in that wheelbarrow."

"It won't fit through this door," Uche said. "The crates scarcely will. But yes, you must bring it all inside. It's not safe where it is."

Lafayette nodded and spun around to grab for the first crate.

It might be easier to just pull out the journals and carry them all inside rather than hauling in the camping supplies with them. But, as much as she wasn't feeling watched at the present moment, she knew that feeling could creep back without warning. Better not to dig around for things meant to be kept hidden. Not in plain sight.

Still, it took four trips to get everything into the house. And Uche wasn't wrong about the narrowness of the doorway. Lafayette had to hold the rectangular crates the long way, keeping her fingers front and back rather than on the sides, and even then she had to tip them a little to get them through.

Luckily, with most of her supplies either empty or consumed, none of the crates were particularly heavy anymore.

Lafayette absorbed the details of the house in snatches as she set each crate down before going back out for the next. The entire space was all one room, although a steep spiral staircase led up to a second story.

The room was lit by a single globe of light hanging from the ceiling in the center of the space. It glowed with a steady, warm light, more like firelight than the electric lights in the streets had been. It made the room, small as it was, feel snug and cozy rather than crowded.

But it was clear that Uche lived alone. There was scarcely room for anyone else.

Uche stayed holding the door until the last crate was inside. Then he closed the door. It clicked shut, but there was no lock or latch.

Even her mother's house back in the village had had a latch. Anyone noticing her mother actually using it would've been highly suspicious of what she was hiding, but she had had a way to keep casual visitors from barging into her home.

Uche had nothing. His house had one door, and that door had no lock.

"I'll get some water for the dog," he said, and shuffled to the far end of the room. This was clearly the kitchen, with a variety of pots and pans hanging from hooks over a worktable of heavy, stained and knife-scarred wood. A single backless stool was drawn up to one side of that table, and Lafayette guessed it was as much dining area as work space.

Uche opened the doors of his only cupboard and took out a soup bowl. He filled it in the sink that stood in the corner of the room, then set it on the floor.

Kora rushed to it with a happy wag of her tail and drank it down in great, loud gulps.

Uche went back to the cupboard for a glass and filled it with water before handing it to Lafayette. Then he ducked into a space tucked out of sight behind the spiral staircase and returned with a second stool.

Lafayette sat down gratefully. She longed to take her boots off, but she knew from experience that once she did that, all the steps of foot hygiene would have to follow. Weeks of walking had taught her a few things, but the importance of taking care of her feet she had learned from her father as soon as she'd left her village.

But that would have to wait. There was too much to be said first.

"You don't trust Margo," she decided to start with.

"I don't trust anyone," he said. And he sounded so tired when he said those words, Lafayette felt it like an ache in her own heart.

"But particularly not her?" Lafayette pressed.

He sighed and rubbed at his face. "I think she means well. But that doesn't make her not dangerous. Quite the opposite, in fact. She could bring danger down without even meaning to. Just the wrong word said to the wrong person... It's all very complicated, Lafayette. There is so much you need to know, and you're going to have to learn it in a hurry."

Then he dropped his hands from his face, and it was like everything about him changed. His posture was straighter, making him taller. The tremble in his hands was gone. He still looked old, but no older than he had looked when she had seen him in her village.

The frailty had been an act. For Margo.

"I have a lot to tell you as well," Lafayette said, a little unnerved by his transformation.

"I gather your mother finally passed," he said, reaching out to grasp her hand warmly once more. "Did your father reach you in time?"

"No," Lafayette said, and felt her throat trying to choke off her words. But she pushed past it. "I did see him. But he's gone now too. That's why I came here. With Kora. I hope that's all right?"

She didn't quite cast a glance around the tiny house again. She didn't want to make him feel bad, if he couldn't let her stay now even though he'd promised.

"You are still very much welcome," he said, giving her hand another squeeze. Then he let her go to reach down and scratch around Kora's ears. "You both are. Although one of us is even more changed than me, aren't we?"

Kora just thumped her tail and leaned in to the scratches.

But Lafayette knew she was waiting for a sign from Lafayette before speaking. A sign she wasn't quite ready to give yet.

"The city is like the village, isn't it?" Lafayette said with a wistful sigh. "Journals have to be hidden, buried out of sight and rarely looked at. And then only under completely security."

"It depends on the journals. But in your case, yes. Your parents left here for a reason," he said with a sigh. "They were being watched. It wasn't safe to stay."

"But you stayed," Lafayette said.

"My circumstances are different," he said, and Lafayette could hear him choosing his words carefully. Hedging. "But also, I'm used to being watched. It's been there, those unseen eyes watching me, almost my entire life. At least since I chose to study history."

"I'm being watched too, I think," Lafayette said.

"What do you mean?" Uche asked sharply.

"Since I came into the city a couple of hours ago. It comes and goes, but I think that's deliberate. Someone, or rather some bunch of kids, has been keeping tabs on me."

"Kids?" Uche said with a frown. "You saw who was watching you, and it was kids?"

"Yeah," Lafayette said. "But, like, street kids. They blended in with the crowds. Except for when I saw them. But the more I think about it, the more I'm sure they wanted me to see them. Is that the same as with you?"

"No," Uche said, chewing at his lip. "That's new. But perhaps not as worrisome. It's possible they just thought you looked like an easy target for theft. Certainly they do not work for Central Planning. Central Planning would never use children in their work. Not even urchins. Never."

"Okay," Lafayette said. She knew that Central Planning was the name for the people who ran things in the capital city, and by extension, throughout the world. And they were the ones who didn't want anyone to know all that her father had discovered in his lifetime.

They were the reason her parents had hid their work. And they were the ones watching Uche now, for signs that he knew what her father had discovered, Lafayette guessed.

But there was so much she didn't know about what any of that actually meant.

"I have so much to tell you," she was just saying again, but before the words were even out, she heard a soft knock at the door behind her. She turned just as the door was swinging open and someone stepped inside.

It was a boy a little older than she was, with tangled waves of reddish-blond hair and skin that was almost more freckle than not. He was wearing the same blue on blue uniform as Margo and the other students. He also had the way of walking Lafayette had seen on some boys in her village, like he'd just shot up a dozen centimeters overnight and was still learning how to move his suddenly longer legs.

Apparently he hadn't seen her or Kora, because he was talking even before he was all the way through the door, and continued talking as he turned to close it behind him.

"Sorry I'm late, Professor. Totally lost track of time. I found a passage in an old farming text that seemed to be about—"

But then he turned back around and finally saw that Uche wasn't alone.

And promptly flushed a deep crimson that was about a third embarrassment and two-thirds outright fear.

"It's all right, Tristan," Uche said. "You can speak freely around Lafayette."

"Lafayette… Eloi," Tristan said, his hazel eyes squinting at her as if asking for confirmation.

"That's me," Lafayette said. She wasn't sure what to make of the fact that he'd apparently heard of her already.

"Tristan Carey is my assistant," Uche told her. "He helps me with historical research. I know I told you to trust no one, but you two can trust each other."

"I thought you were retired?" Lafayette said.

"Only from teaching," Uche said with another tired sort of smile. "The work of history never truly ends. There is always more to uncover and learn from."

"So much more," Tristan said, but under his breath, as if to himself.

"I have enough chicken stew for three," Uche said, pushing up from his stool then waving Tristan to take his place. "I'll heat it up. You two should talk. Get to know each other."

Tristan slid onto the stool, then looked up at her almost shyly. He had the longest lashes Lafayette had ever seen on a boy. "Hi," he said, then flushed again. At least this time it was all embarrassment, no fear.

"Hey," Lafayette said. Kora had come around the worktable to sit pressed up against the side of Lafayette's leg, and Lafayette bent down to pet her absentmindedly. "So you're a historian, studying under Professor Okafo? Like my parents?"

"Not a historian," Tristan said with a shake of his head. "Not yet. I'm still in my first year here."

"Okay," Lafayette said, but she knew it was clear in her voice that she didn't really understand.

"It takes four years of study before you're even allowed to take the entrance exams for one of the colleges," he explained. "Then, if they take you, it's at least another four years before you can take the exit exams. And only if I pass those can I call myself a historian."

"I had no idea it was so complicated," Lafayette said.

"It really isn't," Uche said as he set a steaming bowl of stew in front of each of them, then waved away both of their attempts to get him to take their stools in favor of hunching over his own bowl while standing.

"It's very regimented," Tristan said. "Who is allowed to study what, and who isn't."

"I'm certainly not arguing that isn't true," Uche said as he dug through his stew until he found a herbed dumpling lurking among the pieces of chicken. He ate it with obvious relish before going on. "All I'm saying is, a historian is someone who studies and attempts to learn from history. And you were already doing that before you ever came here. The rest is just… marks on paper."

"I guess," Tristan said.

"The two finest students I ever knew were expelled from this college before even being allowed to sit for their exit exams," Uche said.

Then he glanced at Lafayette significantly.

"My parents?" she asked.

"Your parents, who have done more to advance our knowledge of our past than anyone that Central Planning has given the degree of master historian to in all the years since," Uche said. He raised his spoon to his mouth, but left it hovering there to glance at Tristan. "Although I'm hopeful for the future," he said.

Tristan attempted to appear focused on his own bowl of stew, but Lafayette could see the warm glow that suffused him at Uche's words.

"We're safe here?" Lafayette asked, glancing at the closed but not locked door and at the shuttered window.

"We're safe here," Uche assured her. "I am watched, but not listened to. There are proprieties that are still honored, for now. And as much as I am as a historian, a target of suspicion, I am also still a professor who retired at the end of a distinguished career. My home is safe. You may speak."

Lafayette didn't even know where to start.

But Tristan looked up at her with a very different sort of glow radiating from him this time. He leaned forward with keen interest and said, possibly the very last thing Lafayette would've expected him to say.

"You were there, weren't you?" he said. Despite Uche's assurances of safety, he was whispering. "You were there when the ship went up into the sky."

CHAPTER 8

Lafayette felt like the world was spinning away beneath her.

She had been alone at the edge of that crater when the ship had lifted off. No one else had been anywhere in the area. She and her father had walked for days through entirely unpopulated areas just to get there. The only path that led there was the one her father had worn through the grass on his many trips out there, searching.

No one had been there when the ship had lifted off into the sky save her and Kora.

"There is a college here, not a very large one, but a college all the same," Uche said to her. "They are astronomers. They study the sky. They notice things like a new structure up in orbit, closer than the moons."

"Central Planning has been scrambling to cover it up, the knowledge of that ship," Tristan said. "But they don't have a clue yet what they can call that new light in the sky. All they can do is stop the astronomers from calling it a ship anymore."

"They call it 'the anomaly'," Uche said. "But we all know what they mean."

"We?" Lafayette asked. "Like, everyone?"

"No, not everyone," Tristan said almost sadly. "Just the few of us who dig into things and talk about them together."

"Historians?" Lafayette asked.

"Or other scholars," Uche said. "Like your mother. History was an interest of hers, but botany and medicine were her true loves."

"So much to be learned about medicine from history," Tristan said between bites of stew.

Uche just nodded acceptance of that point.

"So, like, astronomers too?" Lafayette asked.

"The 'we' Uche means is those of us who don't let Central Planning tell us what to think about things," Tristan said, glancing at Uche to see if the professor wanted to take over the conversation. But Uche's attention was focused on finding another dumpling in his stew, so Tristan went on. "It's not any entire colleges, not even history. Lately, especially not history. Central Planning finds people who will see things their way, and those people, regardless of their other talents, always pass the entrance exams."

"But people who question things?" Lafayette asked, afraid she already knew the answer.

"They tend not to make it far at the university," Tristan said. "Not unless they are very, very careful."

"Tristan walks a very fine line," Uche said. "He's too brilliant for even Central Planning to ignore entirely. And yet being assigned to work with me puts him very high on their suspicion list."

"But, without working with you, what's the point?" Tristan said. "I'm here to learn all I can. And you're the only professor willing to teach me what I want to know."

"Which is why you're here now?" Lafayette guessed. "Your real learning doesn't start until the dark of night, far from the eyes of others."

"Yeah," Tristan said, a little taken aback that she'd worked that out.

But Uche just said, "She learned that from her parents too."

"I'd love to know more about what your parents taught you," Tristan said.

"But there are other matters to discuss first," Uche said, finally pushing his empty bowl of stew away and crossing his arms to regard them both. "You saw your father after your mother passed, but he's not with you now."

"No, he's not," Lafayette said, fidgeting with her spoon. "I tried to save him, but it just wasn't possible. I had to run. With Kora. I had to leave him behind."

"Behind where?" Tristan asked.

But Uche just lifted one index finger, up towards the sky. Where, for all Lafayette knew, her father really was just then, passing by on his endless orbiting path.

"On the ship?" Tristan said in a gasping whisper.

"He accidentally turned something on, then he got trapped behind an energy field. It was like a prison cell, I guess? But when he accidentally turned the engines on, he did it wrong. It was a problem. And the only way to fix it was to launch the ship. If we didn't launch the ship, it was going to explode."

Tristan's eyes were wide as he took that all in.

But Uche just said, "We?"

"Yeah," Lafayette said, rubbing at her face. She was so tired. But she really wasn't telling any of this in the right order. "I found three things on board the ship. They were called constructs?" She shot Uche a quick questioning glance.

He just raised his eyebrows in mild surprise. "Constructs? Really?"

"You know what those are?" Lafayette asked.

"They're like ghosts, right?" Tristan put in, looking from his professor to Lafayette and then back again. "Like in the old stories, from the first civilizations. Some of them had constructs they consulted over the course of their early days. The accounts are fragmented and odd, but it sounded like ghosts. Like, ghosts of our ancestors from before we ever came here."

Lafayette's heart skipped a few beats, then rushed to catch up. "You know we're not from here."

"Of course I know we're not from here," he said, and grinned at her. It was a lopsided sort of grin, higher on one side than the other. But it made her feel warmer than even the brightest of Margo's friendly smiles.

It was a grin of conspiracy. It was a grin that meant, we share the same knowledge. We're in the same group.

We're together.

"You found three constructs," Uche said.

"Yes," Lafayette said, dragging her scattered brain back to what she had been saying. "They were teachers, each assigned to a different level of student. The first one, Sameera Adel, she taught me how to speak their language. It's like what you used to speak to my parents in, when you'd visit."

"Of course," Uche said, but there was a hint of wonder in his voice.

"She also taught me how to read," Lafayette said. "The second construct, I didn't get to spend much time with. Because of the problem with the engine. Which I needed the third teacher to help me with. Frank Paine. I left him on when I fled. He's tethered to the desk in his classroom, but he and Sameera were both sure after the ship launched, my father would be free of his cell and could move about the ship. So he'd have company. So... I hope... he's not up there all alone."

"Talking to a construct is like talking to a person?" Tristan asked, leaning forward with keen interest again.

"Um, yeah," Lafayette said, and glanced down at Kora.

Kora looked up at her, tail thumping loudly on the floor behind her.

"Kora is looking different from when I saw her last," Uche said. "She was grayer then. More tired."

"She nearly died when my mother did," Lafayette said, but slowly. She was still making her decision. But she supposed it was inevitable. She had known she was going to do this when she came here in the first place. She was going to tell Uche everything.

And there was no question she was going to tell Tristan all of it, too. If he already knew about the ship and had no problem understanding what all that meant, and greeted it with wonder rather than fear, Kora was perfectly safe with him.

"My father fixed her," Lafayette said, tugging at the ties that kept the grass matting snug around Kora's middle section. Kora gave herself a shake, and the matting pulled free.

"Amazing," Tristan said, immediately jumping off the stool to kneel down by Kora and examine her closely. "These are robotic parts. But she's still organic?"

"She's lots of things," Lafayette said. "My father replaced her heart and other organs to keep her alive. And either that or the paste he gave me to feed her has reversed her aging a bit. The gray is gone from her hair, and she's puppy-like in her energy these days."

"Amazing," Tristan said again, although if anything he infused that word with even more wonder the second time around.

"And what else is she?" Uche asked, clearly knowing that there was more Lafayette hadn't told them yet.

"I couldn't get my father free, or two of the constructs. Their desks were too damaged to get the units out," Lafayette said. "I took Sameera with me, but Kora and I were attacked by a pack of these huge flying cat things as we were running away from the ship. I fell and broke the power unit that made Sameera's construct visible and audible. I couldn't fix it."

"Pity," Uche said. "I would've liked to have met her."

"Well," Lafayette said, licking her lips nervously. But she was committed now. "I couldn't fix the power unit, but it was compatible with the one keeping Kora alive. So I put the other part of the construct, the memory part, inside of Kora. They share her now."

"Share her?" Tristan asked, even as he swept his eyes and his fingertips both all around Kora's middle. Kora even rolled onto her back and splayed her legs out, helping him in his search.

"Part of her is still my mother's dog, Kora," Lafayette said, petting the dog on her head as she spoke. "But the other part is Sameera Adel. Although she prefers to be called Kora now."

"She has the memory of the teacher construct?" Tristan asked, peering into the dog's dark brown eyes as if he could see some other intelligence lurking within their depths.

"More than the memory, I think," Lafayette said. "Her personality too. But it's mixed with Kora a lot. Which is why she prefers to be called Kora now, I guess."

"How does that manifest?" Tristan asked.

As if on cue, Kora rolled back onto her feet. She shook herself off, then looked at Tristan with a steady gaze before saying, "Greetings, Tristan Carey."

Tristan, who had been crouching while he examined the dog, fell back on his butt in surprise.

But Kora just turned her attention to Uche. "And I'm very pleased to meet you, Professor Uche Okafo."

"Likewise," Uche said with the softest of smiles.

But now that she had finally confronted her deepest fear and let others see what Kora really was, Lafayette couldn't let another second pass without speaking her fondest wish.

"We have to rescue my dad," she said. "There has to be a way. There has to be something here in the capital city that will tell us how to get to him."

"Oh," Tristan said, as if something had just dawned on him. But he didn't explain. He just shot an imploring look at Uche.

"Is there something?" Lafayette asked. Her voice was bordering on shrill, but she couldn't quite dial it back down.

Uche just sat with his arms crossed, apparently looking down at the empty stew bowl in front of him. But Lafayette could sense how intensely he was thinking. So she held her tongue and tried hard to practice patience.

For her part, Kora was pressing up against Tristan, looking for more affection from her new friend. He scratched around her ears, but absentmindedly. His eyes, too, were on Uche as Uche ruminated.

"There is almost certainly something," Uche said at last. "But it will be tough knowing where to begin."

"You're being watched more closely now because you left and came back, aren't you?" Lafayette said miserably. "Because of my mom."

Uche raised his eyebrows. "Not just that, Lafayette. I returned, and shortly thereafter, the ship was seen in space that had never been there before. Central Planning, for all their controlling impulses, are still many of the brightest minds among us. They can connect those dots."

"But you didn't have anything to do with it," Lafayette said.

"Not directly, perhaps," he said with a conceding tip of his head. "But your father was following the path I had set him on."

"That had nothing to do with why you were away, though," Lafayette said.

"They don't know that," Tristan said. "I mean, they have no particular reason to be suspicious. Which is why the professor is only being watched, not actively questioned about his activities."

"But it also means other things are being watched more closely now than they were before," Uche said.

"Which is why I'm hunting for historical accounts of the original civilizations in farming texts," Tristan said almost bitterly.

"Everything relevant to our real history is locked up?" Lafayette asked, her heart sinking.

"Not everything, and not forever," Uche said. "Your father is safe, on that ship? For a time, anyway?"

"Frank Paine said he would be," Lafayette said. "It's just… he's all alone up there."

"We will get him down," Uche said. "But it may take some time. We have to do this work in secret, which means it will be slow and cautious, every step of the way. And there will almost certainly be setbacks."

"But we'll help you," Tristan said. "In fact, I think I might have an idea where to start."

"You do?" Lafayette asked, not quite daring to hope.

"Maybe," Tristan hedged. "I have to talk to a friend. It's a long shot. I probably shouldn't have even said anything. But I should go now. If he knows of anything that might help us, I'll come back in the morning and tell you all about it. I mean, either way, I'll come tell you all about it. But for now, I have to run."

"Stay safe," Uche said, saying each word distinctly to be sure it was heard as more than the usual trite message.

"Of course, sir," Tristan said, nodding solemnly.

Then he looked up at Lafayette with a smaller version of that lopsided grin. "I'll see you in the morning. I promise."

Lafayette just nodded. She wasn't used to people making promises to her. Aside from her parents. And her father's promises had been heartfelt, but frequently not kept.

She wasn't entirely sure what to do with the words "I promise" from a stranger.

Tristan gave Kora another pat on the head, then slipped out the door into the night.

That door that still didn't lock.

"My parents' journals are in those crates," Lafayette said to Uche. "Are they safe here?"

Uche gave them a long, ponderous look. Then he heaved a heavy sigh. "No. But they'll have to stay here for tonight. Trying to move them would be riskier than leaving them here."

"What do we do with them tomorrow?" Lafayette asked.

"I don't know. We'll think of something," he said.

Then he broke out of his brooding posture and started gathering the bowls up from the table. "I'm sure you and Kora are both very ready for bed, and completely incapable of getting a lick of sleep. But I have a room ready for you upstairs."

"You do?" Lafayette said.

Uche set the bowls in the sink, then turned to her with a sad smile. "I knew you were coming. I did wonder why you were so delayed. And when the ship appeared in the sky, I wondered… well, a great many things. But I still hoped I would see you. Sooner or later."

He gestured for her to follow him. She glanced at the totes, which felt all too exposed in the middle of the living room. But it was just like every night on the journey here. She had been in a tent, and they had been outside.

The disguise of being totes of ordinary belongings would hold for another night, she guessed. She fetched her satchel, filled with things that she'd need before morning, and latched the lid back down tight.

She made her way up the steep, narrow stairs. Kora followed behind, but Lafayette could tell she was cheating, letting her hover disc carry her with only the softest paddles of her dangling paws to drive her forward, up the stairs.

The upstairs was also all one room, but someone—presumably Uche—had hung a curtain of heavy canvas down the middle. The half that was situated over the front door was clearly his, with books and papers stacked all over a neat little desk, and on a chair beside the desk, and on a table by the little bed, and over every open centimeter of floor all around all those things.

The other side was emptier, but only by comparison. The little bed, night table, and desk and chair took up nearly all the space. But in the corner, directly over the sink in the kitchen, was another sink. Only it was deeper than a sink, more of a washtub. Too small for a bath, but ample for her to wash up in.

She hadn't had a proper washing up since she'd left the ship behind. Only what she could do with a rag and what little water she could spare from her drinking supply.

She was going to be clean. She was going to go to bed clean.

"We'll talk more… well, perhaps not in the morning, but definitely after supper tomorrow," he said. "And I do hope you take Margo up on her offer of a tour and introductions. Whatever happens with your father, you will be here for a while, if not longer. I hope you see some of the good things about the capital city and not just what little company an old man can offer you."

"But is she safe?" Lafayette asked.

Uche considered this carefully. "She may be looking to make a friend. Or she may be an acolyte for Central Planning looking to recruit you. Just be careful what you say. Time will tell. But avoiding her, avoiding people in general, will only bring suspicion on you. And as much as I'd love to just have you spend all your time with Tristan, he does have studies to attend to."

"No, I don't want to be a distraction," Lafayette agreed.

Uche just smiled, a smile whose meaning she knew she wasn't entirely getting.

"I don't think he'd call you that," was all he said.

Then he bid her good night, and went back downstairs.

Leaving Lafayette alone with that washtub, and all the hot water and sweet-smelling soap she could ever want.

Even Kora got a thorough scrubbing.

The hot water really did its work. Not only were they clean before they got into the bed, but despite all her worries, Lafayette fell fast asleep the minute her head touched the pillow.

CHAPTER 9

Lafayette woke up to the sound of something sizzling in the kitchen down below.

And the smell of bacon. She had only ever had bacon while sharing meals with her father on the ship. They had come out fully cooked from a contraption in the wall at the back of his cell that looked like a cupboard. He could slide them out to her through a little drawer, and she'd eaten so many new things she couldn't even name. But her father had recognized bacon from his childhood.

But the minute she heard that sizzling sound, and smelled that bacon smell, she knew the two things would forever be linked in her mind. In a really good way.

She dressed in the clothes she had been keeping for wearing in the city, what had been her festival day clothes back in her home village. Not that she was trying to be fancy, it was just the lightweight materials had been totally impractical for life on the road.

She had no idea what the city had in store for her. But it couldn't possibly have as much tearing and cutting dangers as the grasslands she had just passed through.

She left her sore feet bare. The smooth wood flooring felt good to her blistered and raw skin. As grateful as she'd been for the sturdy boots her father had given her, she was looking forward to finding a looser fitting pair of shoes now.

Not that she had any money left. Or any prospects for work to earn money.

There was a lot she still had to discuss with Uche. She wasn't going to be a dead weight in his house, sucking up resources. But all of that could wait until after she'd had her fill of that bacon.

Kora floated down the stairs behind her just as Uche was lifting a skillet off the heating element and sliding crisp slices of bacon off onto a waiting plate heaped with so much more bacon.

"Your father always loved bacon, and I thought that just might be hereditary," Uche said as she stood there gaping for perhaps a beat too long. But then he smiled at her. "Good morning, Lafayette. Sleep well?"

"Better than I hoped," she said, giving him a questioning look before reaching for any of that bacon. He laughed and nudged the plate closer to her.

"Help yourself," he said, putting the skillet back onto the cook surface and adjusting a knob before cracking eggs onto the pan's already greasy surface. "Traveling is exhausting, but nothing beats that first night back home in my own bed. It almost makes all the nights sleeping on uneven ground worth it."

Lafayette crunched into her first slice of bacon. It was a shade too hot, but she didn't mind.

Then a sudden thought struck her. She put her hand over her mouth as she chewed and swallowed, then said, "I'm sleeping in my dad's bed, aren't I?"

"Indeed," Uche said. "I never married or had children of my own, but I occasionally take in a student who needs a little more of a home touch than the dormitories provide. Your father came here younger than most students, and from much further away. He was struggling, but I could see all the potential just shining out of his eyes. He needed a little more support adapting to university life. And I had the room."

"I know he appreciated it," Lafayette said. "I mean, just apart from all the times you visited, he talked about you a lot."

"He was my favorite student," Uche said. "Not that teachers are supposed to have favorites. And yet. Many of us do."

Lafayette reached for a second piece of bacon. She was just thinking about all the other questions she had about her father, especially her father when he was her age and had lived in this house, when the door was once more briefly knocked on before simply opening up.

She wasn't entirely surprised to see Tristan coming in. But her warm smile of hello froze on her face as he was quickly followed by another boy of about his same age.

This boy was not wearing a school uniform. Far from it: his clothes were a strangely thrown together mix of tight pants he had long since outgrown and nearly worn through with a garishly new, bright red shirt with a sheen to the fabric and far too many glittering buttons.

Most of which he had left open in the front. As if to show off his waifishly thin chest.

His long, unkempt black hair was slicked back from his face, but locks of it were falling forward, and even as she watched him toss his head to throw it all back out of his eyes again, she could tell by the practiced quality to that gesture that he did this all the time.

But none of that bothered her as much as his eyes. They were a brown so dark the pupils and irises blended together. And they were narrowed a bit as he focused on her in the relative darkness of the house interior after being out in the bright light of day outside.

There was something familiar about those eyes. Not their appearance. She didn't think she'd ever seen those eyes before in her life. And, dark as they were, she knew if she had, she would remember.

No, what felt familiar was the way he was looking at her. The way he was *watching* her.

The way it felt when he was watching her.

She knew it was paranoid, and maybe even crazy. But she was sure those eyes had been among those watching her the night before.

She glanced down at Kora, then nudged the dog with her foot to get her out of view from the still open door. Kora wasn't wearing her grass mat. Her metallic core was on full display.

Uche turned toward the door with the skillet of scrambled eggs in his hand. He seemed to be thinking the same thing as Lafayette, as his smile of greeting for Tristan morphed into a frown of disapproval.

"Door, Dieter," Tristan said to the other guy, then slid back onto the stool he'd been sitting on the night before. Like they were resuming that former meal, with each of them in their places once more.

Dieter shut the door, then leaned against it with his hands in his pockets. A picture of casualness. But a little too artfully casual for Lafayette's liking.

"Eat up, Lafayette," Uche said as he slid her portion of the eggs onto her plate.

"You know who this is?" Lafayette asked him. She didn't even bother to whisper.

Dieter, leaning against the door, sneered but said nothing.

"He's a friend of Tristan's," Uche said. But if there was more meaning in those words, like any idea of what Uche thought of this friend, his tone conveyed none of it.

"My best friend," Tristan said. "I'll share my eggs with him."

"There's enough here for four," Uche said, and turned to fetch another plate from his cupboard.

Tristan motioned for Dieter to join them at the table. Dieter seemed to consider refusing for a moment. But Lafayette couldn't entirely blame him if the smell of all that bacon made it impossible. She was sure she couldn't have turned away, even if she hadn't been as starving as she still was.

She dug into the eggs between bites of bacon and found them every bit as flavorful as her mother always made them back home. Maybe she'd even learned the technique from Uche. They were infused with bacon-flavor, but there was also a medley of herbs involved, only a few she could actually name.

"Sorry, I really needed that," Tristan said after bolting down his share of the food in record time. "But I wanted to tell you what I've been up to since last night."

"Not sleeping," Uche said. An observation.

"No, and I have a class in half an hour," Tristan said with a little wince. "I'll be fine. But first, Dieter has some leads on where we can look for ways to help your dad."

"You told him about my dad?" Lafayette asked. More aggressively than she had intended.

"He already knew about the ship," Tristan said with a shrug. "And he knows as much about the real history of this world as I do."

"Because *he* won't shut up about it," Dieter said between bites of egg. But the quick glance he shot at Tristan was, even Lafayette had to admit, one of fondness.

"Yeah," Tristan said with another shrug. "Partly it's because I just love talking about it. But also, sometimes Dieter finds stuff. And he brings it to me. And it's always interesting."

"Historical stuff?" Lafayette guessed.

"Historical stuff," Dieter repeated. Lafayette couldn't quite tell if he was making fun of her or not.

"Yeah," Tristan said, reaching for another slice of bacon. If he noticed the mood between Lafayette and Dieter, he didn't say anything about it.

"The first thing we have to do is get those totes out of the house," Uche said. "They are dangerous. They must be kept safe."

"Dangerous?" Tristan said, looking at the totes for the first time. "What's in them?"

"I'd rather not say," Lafayette said, crossing her arms and not quite looking at Dieter.

"You don't have to tell me," Dieter said. "I'm just the guy who'll be helping you hide them, is all. I don't care what's in them."

"Oh, really?" Lafayette said. "That's big of you. As if I'd believe for a minute you'd hide something for me and not look inside the minute my back was turned."

"I kind of doubt I'd find anything in there to interest me," he said. Then his eyes swept over Lafayette rather than the totes, and she was suddenly unsure precisely what he was referring to. But she didn't like the way those eyes felt on her. Not at all.

"Diet?" Tristan said, sounding confused.

"I'll help," Dieter said. "It's what I do. Right?"

"If you're helping, you have a right to know, I think," Tristan said. But he looked to Uche for confirmation.

Uche's face remained impassive.

But Dieter just shrugged again. "Look, I don't even care. I'm sure it's more historical stuff. And I've had my fill. But I'll help you hide it. Then we can discuss the other thing."

"Don't you have class?" Lafayette asked.

"I do," Tristan said. Then he gave Dieter an imploring look. "You can help her without me, right?"

Lafayette was about to object, but Uche beat her to it. "No, best not to move things in broad daylight. Not to and from this house, anyway."

"Agreed," Dieter said. "It has to wait until after dark. I have some… friends making a delivery to the cafeteria. They're going to be running late, I think. We'll swing by here and add your stuff to the mix, then separate it out again at the other end."

"I don't get it," Lafayette said.

"I get a weekly delivery of food," Uche said. "It won't look strange, even after dark."

"And I can match those totes. No one is going to notice when we make the switch," Dieter said.

"But where are you taking them?" Lafayette asked.

"Somewhere safe," Dieter said, sounding exasperated.

"You'll know where they are," Tristan assured her. "It won't be smart for you to go back and forth all the time, but you'll know where they are. We can get you to them whenever you need them."

Lafayette looked at Uche, but he just looked right back at her. Apparently, the decision about her parents' things was hers.

Only really it wasn't. Because there was no way she was putting Uche in danger.

But she really hated the idea of being separated from all she had left of her parents. She practically had those journals memorized. She could redraw and rewrite most of the pages herself if she needed to.

She just liked touching the pages they had touched. And looking at her mother's sketches and her father's schematics in their vastly different art styles.

"Okay," she said.

"Great!" Tristan said, and gave Dieter a nudge. "I have to run to class, and Dieter has business of his own to get to. But we'll be back to move the totes tonight. And then I'll tell you what we're thinking, about how to get to your dad."

"Great," Lafayette said. She was echoing his word, but she couldn't quite echo his enthusiasm.

Dieter glanced at her one last time before the two of them headed out the door, but it only made her more sure than before. He had definitely been watching her move through town the night before.

And the friends he was calling on to help them move her parents' things? They were likely attached to other pairs of eyes that had been watching her.

"You said not to trust anyone," Lafayette said to Uche after the two boys had gone.

"I did," Uche said. "And yet, all too often, you have to. We can't do everything on our own. All I can tell you is what I told you before. Dieter's friends are like the street kids you saw last night. They may be trouble, but they aren't Central Planning. And right now, trouble that isn't Central Planning is trouble I can handle. *We* can handle," he stressed, and gave Lafayette's shoulder a reassuring squeeze.

Lafayette wished she could be half so confident. But she just felt unmoored in a way even a belly heavy with bacon and eggs didn't help with.

CHAPTER 10

Lafayette had no idea what she was going to do to fill an entire day. She couldn't leave the house, not until she knew the journals were safely hidden. When she went out with Kora, she saw that the wheelbarrow she had left outside had already disappeared sometime during the night or early in the morning. There was no way she was leaving those totes unguarded.

And she hoped Dieter's plan involved putting them somewhere she felt they were truly secure. Or she was going to have to make a scene. And she really didn't want to do that.

So exploring the area by the light of day was out of the question, for at least one more day. But after helping Uche with the dishes, she was left with not a single thing to do.

She hadn't anticipated how quickly boredom would set in now that she wasn't walking all day. She had rather thought her feet would have time to heal before she got restless again.

"Lafayette," Uche said. He had gone up to his room after they'd finished with the dishes, and she had assumed he was starting his work for the day. But now he was coming back down the stairs.

With something in his hands.

"A gift for you," he said, handing her a truly massive book. The cover was a soft brown leather, still warm from his own hands. The stacked pages were thicker than her fist, but the paper was fine.

There had to be a thousand pages in that book. And every one of them was blank, waiting for her to fill it.

"Seriously?" Lafayette asked, even as he held out a small pouch for her also to take. She opened it to see a thick-tipped pen, a fine-tipped pen, and a mechanical pencil.

"You only have a day, and you'll have to be careful about what you commit to this book from the others," he said with a nod towards the totes. "But this is not my office hours day. There will be no visitors. You will be safe to work at the table there, copying all that you can before dark."

"Thank you," Lafayette said, fighting to blink back tears. "I have a journal of my own, but it's nearly full. And it's not half so nice as this book."

He smiled at her fondly. "Do let me know when this one, too, is nearly full. I'll be sure to get you another before you run out of pages."

"That must be years away," Lafayette said, flipping through the blank pages and drawing in a lungful of the fresh smell from the untouched paper.

"Just be careful what you choose to record," he said again. Then with a little nod either to her or to himself—Lafayette wasn't sure which—he went back up to the desk in his half of the upstairs room.

Lafayette opened the first tote, dug down past the cooking utensils to the pair of wrapped journals at the bottom, and pulled them both out. Then she perched on the stool, bare feet hooked through the rungs of the stool legs, and turned to the first page of her journal before unwrapping her father's book of schematics.

It contained everything she would need to know about Kora and how she worked. She had studied these pages more than any of the others, but she copied them down again, anyway. Out of everything she was about to hide away, this was the information she was more likely to need than any other.

Kora paced the room nervously for a few minutes. But then she flopped down on a rug near the door, almost blocking the door, although Lafayette guessed this was more about the comfort of the rug compared to the bare wood floor than an effort to guard the house.

Either way, within two blinks of an eye, the dog was snoozing with the softest of snores. That, plus the sound of Lafayette's pen tips on the fine-grained paper, were the only sounds in the house. Whatever Uche was up to upstairs, it was a silent activity.

Although the world outside of the house was far from silent. She could hear people moving around. From the laughter and loud voices carrying over a distance of winding streets, she was sure she was hearing students moving through that grassy field. It was a pleasant sound, though. It reminded her of long, hot, lazy days back home.

Uche set a plate of bread, cheese, and a sliced red apple by her elbow for lunchtime, but Lafayette pressed on with her work, only taking bites of food as she turned to a fresh page.

The light from the sun faded and the light from the glowing globe overhead grew at a matching rate, so Lafayette didn't exactly notice when night had fallen. She had a vague sense of being hungry again, lunch being a very old memory.

But what brought her out of her focused work was the cramp in her hand that was becoming impossible to ignore. Finally, she just had to lay her pen aside, unable to go on.

"A welcome change from being footsore, I imagine," Uche said as he saw her massaging her own hand.

"I didn't get as much done as I wanted," she said, wishing she could wring a few more pages out of that wreck of a hand but knowing it wasn't going to be possible. Even if she could power through, she was out of time.

"That was inevitable, I'm afraid," Uche said. "The boys will be here soon. You should be ready to go."

Lafayette wanted to groan aloud at that. It meant cramming her feet back into her socks and boots. And as much as her socks were all clean now, and after hanging from the edges of the washbasin since morning were surely dry as well, being barefoot all day had felt really good.

"I hope we don't have to go far," she said as she headed for the stairs to get her socks and boots.

"No, I don't imagine Dieter will want to hide anything too far for you to keep an eye on it," Uche said, moving to the bottom of the stairs so that he could keep talking to her as she went up and then back down again. "How he and Tristan ever fell in together, neither of them has ever told me. But I know they trust each other like brothers. And in this city, that's saying something. Tristan's family is one of the wealthiest trading families in the city. Certainly the wealthiest family with no ties to Central Planning."

"And Dieter?" Lafayette asked. She got her socks on without incident, but pulling on those boots involved more than a little wincing.

"So far as I know, Dieter grew up on the streets," Uche said. "All too common, and seemingly more common by the day. It's a problem."

"So he's an orphan?" Lafayette asked. All too aware she was half an orphan herself.

"Or his parents are alive but have no interest in him," Uche said. "That's all too common as well."

"But we have to trust him?" Lafayette asked, looking at the totes in a way she was sure was too much like wistful.

"Tristan already does," Uche said. "And I trust Tristan."

"Right," Lafayette said.

She didn't think her trust worked in a chain like that. But she wasn't going to argue about it with Uche.

"Kora should stay here with me," Uche said.

"What? Why? I can put her cover back on her," Lafayette said, all in a rush.

"No, there's no need to cover her up," Uche said. "Her body isn't the problem. Being half robot and half real dog is unique, but the sight of her wouldn't be completely unusual."

"She eats a nutritive paste," Lafayette said.

But Uche was already nodding his understanding. "Yes, I know precisely what your father mixed up for her. It's only for her organic parts, not her robotic ones. It's a tonic the biology students here use for their animals when they are ill or undernourished. Specifically created for maintaining unusual animals like Kora. I can get you more of it."

"That's a relief," Lafayette said. "But why does she have to stay with you, then?"

"What you're doing is not illegal, but it is highly suspect. If you're detained or questioned, Kora might just be one question too many. If they stop you kids on your own, I'm sure you'll be able to explain yourselves well enough, to talk your way out of trouble. But if Kora were with you, she might be one thing too much to explain. It's just safer if she's here with me."

"Okay," Lafayette said. "She'll talk your ear off, I think. She's been bored all day while I've been working."

"I wasn't bored precisely," Kora said from where she was apparently still napping on the rug by the door. But then she opened a single eye and looked up at them both. "I was very tired, from all the walking. It feels good not to walk today."

"Says the girl who was cheating for most of it," Lafayette said. Then she stage-whispered to Uche, "She uses her floating disc to carry most of the weight for her."

"Indeed," Uche said.

Kora just grinned up at them both with a doggy grin.

She scurried out of the way at the first hint of Tristan's brisk knock, just avoiding the door as it swung open immediately after. Tristan and Dieter were standing there, but they stepped aside to let two smaller kids squeeze between them. They were each carrying a tote which they brought to the worktable near the kitchen.

"Can you consolidate what you need to hide down to two totes?" Dieter asked as Uche directed the two kids in leaving the totes of food stores on the floor by the back of the stairs rather than on his worktable.

"I guess," Lafayette said. Tristan helped her open all the lids, and she shifted the contents. All the journals in one tote, and the last of her father's artifacts in another. That left her with the camping equipment and the cooking utensils as well as her clothes and things to keep at Uche's house.

Or, more likely, sell them for money to buy a new pair of shoes and maybe some new clothes.

"Ready?" Tristan asked. She stood back with a nod. Then Dieter pointed for the kids to pick up Lafayette's totes and hustle back outside with it. Her totes were so much lighter—even the one full of journals was still more than half empty space under that lid—that Lafayette supposed to an outside observer, it really would look like they'd unloaded the food stores from the other totes and were now carrying the empties back outside again.

Not that she knew anyone was watching. When she peered out the door, the only feeling of eyes on her was from Dieter, and from one of the two kids.

"Ready," Lafayette said.

Kora barked and thumped her tail, and Lafayette had to appreciate that Kora was still being discreet about where she spoke out loud and in whose company.

But she really wished she had thought to say goodbye to her before the boys had arrived. Now it was too late.

"I'll be back soon," she said, scratching around the dog's ears.

Then she was outside in the cool night air, standing with Tristan and Dieter.

And it felt really, really weird. Kora had always been her mother's dog. Her mother's shadow. Up until the day her mother died. But since then, she had been Lafayette's shadow.

Lafayette could only guess at the day when that had stopped being annoying. And she had no idea at all when it had become something that left a real sense of loss now that it wasn't there.

"You okay?" Tristan asked.

"Fine," Lafayette said, and tried not to look as freaked out as she felt.

"Are you worried about your dad?" he asked.

But Dieter blew out an irritated breath. "Can we get this done first and then talk about our feelings?"

"Diet," Tristan said in a chastising tone.

"No, he's right," Lafayette said. "Let's go. I don't like feeling this exposed."

"This way," Dieter said, and led them to where the other two kids waited. They had her totes stacked up on a wheelbarrow, perched precariously atop six others.

It took a minute before Lafayette realized it was *her* wheelbarrow.

"That was gone before," she said.

"Obviously," Dieter said. "I needed it for the plan."

"So you just took it without asking me?" she said.

Dieter said nothing. It was hard to tell in the unlit darkness, but she was pretty sure he was smirking at her.

But they pressed on, through a couple twists of narrow roads, east towards the university but further north than the library where she had met Margo. The building they ended up at had just as large a footprint as the library, but it was not so imposingly high. There were more doors, lots more windows, and light was spilling out of it onto another square of foot-worn grass.

"Cafeteria," Tristan whispered to Lafayette. "It's open until midnight, and there's usually a lot of students in there kind of studying, but mostly not really. I usually eat at the professor's house myself, though."

"Must be nice, having to choose between two free meals," Dieter tossed back over his shoulder. But before either of them could respond, he pointed to a smaller path that wound around to the back of the building, then down a small hill to a door that had to lead into the basement under the cafeteria.

"Knock twice," Dieter said, and the kid who wasn't driving the wheelbarrow scurried forward to knock on that door. It opened up almost at once and a girl with long, dark hair pulled into a topknot poked her head out to peer out at them. She was wearing a student's uniform, minus the jacket, but with a large apron covering the rest of it.

"Delivery?" she asked in a bored voice. "Kind of late, isn't it?"

"Long day," Dieter said, then slipped something to her that Lafayette didn't see. The girl looked at whatever it was nestled in her palm, then smiled widely before throwing the door open.

The doorway was more than big enough for the entire wheelbarrow to pass through. If the girl thought it was odd that they were bringing the entire wheelbarrow into her storage room, she didn't say a thing. She just stuck whatever it was in the pocket of her pants under all the folds of that apron, then went back about her business.

"This way," Dieter said, leading the wheelbarrow and the others past shelf after shelf of foodstuffs, all the way to the very back wall of the basement. As they went, one kid was pushing the wheelbarrow but the other was taking out totes and setting them on shelves as they wheeled by. Soon the only totes still in the wheelbarrow were the two of Lafayette's things. And where they stopped was right under the front steps, Lafayette was sure.

But she wasn't sure why they stopped there, of all places. Still, she didn't ask. She just watched as Dieter pulled a single key on a ring out of his pocket and stuck it into what appeared to be the mortar between two stone blocks.

Lafayette heard a click, and then the blocks themselves swung forward. It was a door, a door disguised to look just like the wall itself. But beyond that door was nothing but darkness.

"This hidey-hole for illicit goods isn't currently in use," Dieter said, even as he waved the kid with the wheelbarrow to put the entire load into that darkness. "The door at the back is always open, although not everyone doing a work study here is as cool as Liana. You'll have to pick your moment, if you want to get back in here."

Lafayette tried to see how deep the hole was, but it was impossible to tell. The kid just wheeled the barrow in until there was enough room to shut the door behind it, then stepped back out of the way so Dieter could do just that.

Then he turned the key back with a resounding click, jiggled it free from the hidden lock, and handed the key and ring both to Lafayette.

"Thank you," she said as she took the key from him.

"You can't come here a lot, or the secret won't keep," Dieter said. "And as much as I don't want to know what's in it, I reckon that's because it's a pretty big secret."

"That's right," Tristan said. Then he cast a nervous glance at the two kids, for which Lafayette was grateful. It meant she didn't have to bring it up.

"These two won't blab," Dieter said, even as he grabbed one of the two kids, put them in a headlock, and rubbed his knuckles aggressively against the top of the kid's head until every strand of their fine brown hair was standing on end.

"You're sure?" Tristan asked.

"Handpicked by me," Dieter said, a little more soberly than before. "They're solid."

"We won't tell nobody," the smaller of the two kids said. They might have been a girl. It was hard to tell.

All of them made their way back out of the maze of food shelves, then through the door and back out into the night.

Only that back alley was less empty than it had been just a moment before. Someone was standing there, just under the globe of light. Looking for all the world like she'd been waiting for them.

It was Margo.

CHAPTER 11

"Hey!" Margo said brightly as she saw Tristan's face by the light of the globe. Her gaze passed over Dieter and the two kids with mild confusion before landing on Lafayette. Then she lit up even more than before. "Hi, Lafayette! Were you eating here with your friends?"

"No," Lafayette said, then instantly regretted it. She had no idea what sort of cover story would make sense here. Eating was probably the best one. Although why they would be coming out of the basement would still need explaining.

But Tristan felt her distress at once and took a half a step closer to Margo. "I was just giving her a little tour. I thought my sister Brooke was working in supply tonight and we were going to say hi, but she's not here."

"No, she doesn't do cafeteria duty anymore," Margo said. "I've reassigned her to more home visits. I was swamped, and the retired professors like her nearly as well as they like me."

"That's good," Tristan said. "Good for Brooke."

"You two know each other, then?" Lafayette asked. She only mentally noted that Margo didn't know Dieter at all, which made how close she was to Tristan an open question, if she'd never met his best friend.

"Not well," Margo said, almost as if she were answering the question Lafayette hadn't asked. "Our families have known each other for generations, though. We're practically cousins."

"Except for that part about not being related at all," Dieter said dryly.

"Well," Margo said, her eyes darting to and then quickly away from Dieter. So Lafayette wasn't the only one who found his intensity a little unsettling. That was actually comforting, in a way. "We probably are related, if you go far enough back."

"If you go far enough back, we're all related," Tristan said, catching Lafayette's eye if just for a split second.

But it wasn't like what he said wasn't true. She knew every human on this planet had evolved on some other, unknown planet. But they'd still all come from the same place, originally. At least, her father had always said so.

They really all were related, if you went far enough back. They just didn't come from families that originated here.

Lafayette noticed that Dieter was smirking at her again, although she had no idea why.

"It's good that I ran into you, actually," Margo said, and swung a book bag that had been resting against the back of her hip forward so she could dig through it. "I was hoping to stop by Professor Okafo's house today, but he's on the schedule as do not disturb, no office hours, so I didn't."

"His study time is something he defends vigorously," Tristan said.

"I know," Margo said, with the air of someone who had found that out the hard way. She smiled up into Tristan's eyes for a beat, then turned her attention back to digging through her bag. "Ah, here it is," she said, and thrust a pouch into Lafayette's hands before Lafayette even realized it was happening.

"What's this?" Lafayette asked. Then she brought it up to her nose and sniffed. Even through the canvas sides of the pouch she could smell the sharp scent of ginger, and the subtler but still potent smell of turmeric.

"My grandmother's tea," Margo said anyway. "I don't think I'm going to be able to stop by for a few more days, but you can bring that to him for me, right? It's just the thing for the aches he gets in his joints. That last journey really took it out of him."

"My mother was dying," Lafayette said.

"Oh, I know! I'm so sorry! I wasn't blaming you," Margo said, and grabbed Lafayette's arm in that hugging away again. "And he's doing better. Especially now that he has someone staying with him. He's always better with company."

"I'm there every night," Tristan said.

"Oh, I know," Margo said, and switched her hugging arm gesture over to him. "You're a dear."

"He's my professor," Tristan said, flushing a bit.

"I know, I know," Margo said. "Still, you take fine care of him. I know you do. He's been so much more alert since your other professor switched your mentorship over to Professor Okafo."

"Our interests are more closely aligned," Tristan said. "Professor Milton is a sociologist, but Professor Okafo is a proper historian."

"Sure, sure," Margo said, but with the air of someone who's stopped really listening. "I'm sorry to rush off, but I really have somewhere to be. Lafayette! You can bring that tea to the professor?"

"Of course," Lafayette said.

"Great. And I'll see you later this week?"

"If you're visiting the professor, I'm sure I'll be there," Lafayette said.

"And Kora too," Margo said. "Such a beautiful dog. A little bit in need of a bath, though," she added with a wince of apology.

"She's had one," Lafayette said.

"Great!" Margo said, her face all friendly brightness again. "I really do have to go. But I hope Tristan didn't give you the *full* tour. I was really looking forward to taking you around."

"It was very brief," Tristan said.

And Dieter, to Lafayette's surprise and annoyance, barked out a loud laugh at that.

But Margo just gave him a single puzzled glance before deciding anyone dressed that way wasn't worth paying much attention to.

"I'll see you both around, then," she said with a wave, then jogged back out of the alley towards the front of the cafeteria.

"Why was she here?" Dieter asked. He almost spat those words out, they were delivered so aggressively.

"For the tea?" Lafayette said, but slowly. She had no real idea.

"It's possible," Tristan said with a shrug to Dieter. "Her grandmother makes it in big batches, and Margo delivers it to a lot of the retired professors. It's not crazy, the idea that she stores it here at the cafeteria. She probably has a couple of shelves for her own use. Well, her own department's use."

"Sure," Dieter said, and Lafayette thought he was prepared to drop the matter. But they were no more than ten steps back towards Uche's house when he added, "She did a lot of digging in that bag, though. For something she had just dropped in there."

But one of the two kids spoke next. Not that it was particularly illuminating. They just gave a grumbled, "Bags, man."

But Lafayette got it. She had often found the thing she had just put into her satchel was the last thing to come to hand. It happened.

And yet, her gut had the same question as Dieter, now that he'd pointed it out.

"That felt like a setup," Tristan sighed. "But why?"

"Someone's watching the new girl," Dieter said airily.

"More than one someone," Lafayette grumbled back.

But he took her angry look with his usual careless attitude. "Sure. You're interesting. You draw the eye. Even without your dog with you."

"That's why you've been watching me? Because I'm interesting and draw the eye?" Lafayette demanded.

"Wait, what?" Tristan said, sounding genuinely confused.

"You two, scram," Dieter said with a dismissive wave, and the two kids disappeared into the shadows faster than should technically be possible.

"What's going on, Dieter?" Tristan asked his friend. There was an edge to his voice that Lafayette hadn't heard there before.

But Dieter didn't seem bothered by it. "You know what I do."

"And why you do it," Tristan added. "But still. Explain this. Why have you been watching Lafayette? She's no danger to your people."

"She's been shedding questionable tech for weeks all the way up the trunk road," Dieter said with a vague wave in Lafayette's direction. Like she wasn't really part of this conversation. "Lots of people have been watching her."

"And?" Lafayette said pointedly.

"Well, now that I know you're mixed up in Uche Okafo business, I'm definitely going to be keeping eyes on you," Dieter said.

"Why?" Tristan asked. He sounded like someone making an effort to keep his patience.

"Because *you're* mixed up in Uche Okafo business," Dieter said. "And I don't think I need to tell you what happens to his most favored students. Over and over again."

"They get expelled if they're not careful," Tristan said.

"They *all* get expelled," Dieter said. "There is no amount of careful that stops that from happening. And for some of them, it only starts there. Some of them, they're just never seen here again."

"Like my parents," Lafayette said.

But Dieter was already shaking his head at her. "No, your parents were the smart ones. They weren't expelled. They just left. With their lives."

"How many students could Professor Okafo have had?" Tristan mused. "I mean, students like you mean it."

"Too many," Dieter said. "And I've checked. In records you won't be able to find in the aboveground world. But I can show you, if you really want to know."

He said that last bit like it was the direst threat he had ever laid down.

And, from the way the color rushed out of Tristan's face, he heard it that way too.

"Would you show me?" Lafayette asked. Because she was willing to take up his challenge.

"Maybe," Dieter said, giving her a look like he found her equal parts mysterious and amusing.

She didn't really like that look either.

"We should get back," Tristan said, catching Lafayette's elbow in one hand and Dieter's in the other and propelling them back up the hill to the plaza in front of the cafeteria.

"So I'm being watched," Lafayette said as they walked. "I get that. But that doesn't explain Margo standing outside that door."

"Doesn't it?" Dieter shot back. "I suspect she was following us. Ineptly. And she got caught when we came back out faster than she thought we would."

"Margo Weiss," Tristan said with deep skepticism.

"Whatever her name is," Dieter said. But with the air of someone who knew one hundred percent that was her name.

"Margo Weiss, oldest daughter of Maury Weiss, judge of the high court," Tristan went on.

Dieter just shrugged.

"She's too prominent to be a spy?" Lafayette guessed.

"No one is too prominent to be a spy," Dieter said in a low growl.

But Tristan threw a sideways glance at Lafayette and gave her a quick nod.

"I saw that," Dieter grumbled.

"Margo told me she likes to be helpful," Lafayette said.

"And she does," Tristan readily agreed. "But in big, grand gestures. Spying? Something where no one will ever credit her with anything she does? That's not her style."

"You make her sound a little… mercenary?"

That wasn't quite the word she wanted, but Tristan was shaking his head anyway. "I've known Margo since we were babies. I've known Margo longer than I've known Dieter here," he added, ignoring Dieter's answering scowl.

"But she said she didn't know you well," Lafayette said.

"Well caught," Dieter said, but she wasn't really in the mood for a compliment from him.

"I think she really was just looking for you, to get the tea to Uche. Because she wouldn't risk violating his do not disturb day a second time," Tristan said. "There's no reason to make it complicated. It's exactly what she would do. In the service of being helpful."

Which all sounded perfectly reasonable to Lafayette. And she was just letting it soak in and ease the tight knots her stomach had been forming.

But Dieter had to ruin it by mumbling under his breath, "That's why it's such a good cover story, you see. Even her oldest friends would believe it. Top-notch spy craft. Seriously. I just might find myself admiring her for it."

Tristan scowled, but said nothing. And they let the matter drop the rest of the walk back to Uche's place.

CHAPTER 12

The alley leading up to Uche's door was filled with the smell of Lafayette's mother's pan bread. The herbs she used in the dough, the sharper smell of the cheese she sprinkled on top, but strongest of all the oil she always fried it in, crisping up the edges and infusing the whole disc-shaped wonder in rich flavor.

For a moment, Lafayette thought she was dreaming. She hadn't had her mother's pan bread in months, although she had craved it more than once.

But then she saw the grin on Tristan's face and knew he was smelling it too.

"Uche's pan bread," he said. "You're in for a treat. He only makes it when he's making chicken and okra stew, and that's not something he whips up every day."

"My mother made chicken and okra stew, especially on our birthdays," Lafayette said. "I suppose she got the recipe from Uche."

"You'll have to tell me how they compare," Tristan said, and jogged ahead to open the door for all of them.

But then he noticed that Dieter was hanging back, as if reluctant to leave the shadows.

"Diet?" he said.

"I gotta go," Dieter said. "It smells amazing, enjoy. But I have work to do."

"What kind of work?" Lafayette asked, perhaps a touch too aggressively. But when she reached inside the pocket of her pants, she could feel the key on the ring he had given her, still there. So her parents' journals were safe.

"You know what work I have to do," Dieter said. "Honestly, we're standing in an open street."

"An empty open street," Tristan put in.

"No, I get it," Lafayette said, keeping her voice low. "Just because we don't see anyone there doesn't mean we're alone."

"Now she gets it," Dieter said, throwing up his hands in a theatrical gesture.

"What do you mean *now* I get it?" she demanded. "I've been keeping secrets my entire life. I know not to take anything for granted."

"Do you?" Dieter said, raising a single eyebrow at her skeptically.

"Diet," Tristan said, a gentle warning that Dieter ignored.

"You just met me," Lafayette said, moving closer to Dieter so she could growl up into his smug, condescending face.

She hated the fact that he was taller. But most people were.

"Yes, we just met," Dieter said. "But I've known you were coming for quite some time. Do you have any idea how rare the things are you've been dropping behind you like breadcrumbs to mark your trail? How many people would talk about their sudden appearance in the trading world?"

"What do you mean?" Lafayette asked. But she was afraid she already knew what he meant. And that he was right.

But he kept explaining anyway. "The people you traded with, most of them didn't know what you gave them. Sure. I guess you were *careful* about that."

His disdain had been apparent enough without him hitting the word so hard it made Lafayette flinch.

But he wasn't done yet. "But you were trading with caravan people. And even if they don't know what you gave them, they all know who to take weird things to. For a better price than they paid you. Your load of goods has been quite a boon to the trunk road economy these last few weeks."

"I needed food," Lafayette said. She hated how small her voice sounded just then. But she hated even more how small she felt.

She hadn't known. She had been drawing all sorts of attention, and she hadn't even had a clue.

"My people have been keeping track of you for weeks, watching your progress and scooping up what they could of what you were leaving behind you. For a price, but we still managed to acquire most of it," Dieter said.

"Who are your people?" Lafayette asked.

But to her surprise, it was Tristan that lunged for her, grasping her arm in both of his hands and whispering close to her ear. "Not here. Not out loud."

"Those kids? Those are your people?" Lafayette pressed on despite the growing smirk on Dieter's face. "You get to be king of the little kid gang?"

The something else clicked. He said he'd been watching her on the road. No, not him. His people.

His kids.

Those kids in the caravan. They *had* been watching her too closely.

"You know nothing about life in the capital city," Dieter said. "I'm starting to think you're not much up on life anywhere on this planet. But whatever. My point still stands that I have to go. Go, enjoy your dinner. Stay out of trouble, if you can. I'll be back."

Those last three words were directed at Tristan, who just nodded.

It was only after Dieter had melted into the shadows and flitted away that Tristan looked down and saw he was still gripping Lafayette's arm. And standing so close his face was brushing against the hair of her bun.

"Sorry," he mumbled, stepping back.

She followed him into the house and was immediately tackled by an overjoyed Kora. The dog only just managed to wait until Tristan had closed the door before bursting into human voice.

"I waited so long! You were gone forever! We haven't been apart since I met you, and I was so worried you were never coming back!"

she said, all in a rush. Lafayette wasn't even sure how she got all those words out, since she never slowed in her frantic licking and pawing all over Lafayette as she did so.

"Her dog nature is strong," Uche commented with a smile in his voice as he turned from his cooktop to set a plate heaped high with steaming pan bread on the middle of the worktable.

"I'm sorry. I forgot myself," Kora said, and sat down neatly on the floor.

"I missed you too, Kora," Lafayette assured her, and bent over to use both hands to scratch all around the dog's ears.

But then she hustled over to the table as Uche turned again with bowls heaped with chicken and okra stew, liberally garnished with some chopped green herbs. Cilantro, maybe, or parsley. It could be either. Her mother had always adjusted the recipe to what she had on hand.

Lafayette took a bite. Parsley, but a sharper variety than Lafayette was used to. It brought out the flavors in the broth, which also contained a handful of brown rice. Not her mother's recipe, then, but still good.

"Dieter couldn't stay?" Uche asked halfway to reaching for another bowl.

"No, he needs to follow up on our lead," Tristan said. "But what Lafayette brought with her is safe now. So that's okay."

Lafayette felt her face flushing at the thought of how careless she had apparently been, but she said nothing and kept eating her stew.

"He is cautious, that one," Uche said as he brought his own bowl to the table. He had gotten a third stool from somewhere and was sitting on it now. It was taller than the other two stools, and he was taller than both of them by quite a bit. It was like sitting at a table with a giant from a children's story, like he wasn't even on the same scale as the two of them.

"He is," Tristan said. He threw the smallest of glances across the table at Lafayette, and she put her spoon down in dismay.

"I didn't know," she said. "I thought I was being careful, but I guess I really wasn't. But I didn't have enough food, and there was no work I could do that was of any use to anybody. I know because I asked. So many times."

"What's all this?" Uche asked.

"I didn't mean it like that," Tristan said. "Honestly, Lafayette. I didn't mean it like that."

"Dieter meant it like that," Lafayette said.

"He was just being…" Tristan said, but words failed him. He looked down at his half-eaten stew, as if he could find what he wanted to say there amongst the chicken.

"He feels threatened," Uche guessed.

"By me?" Lafayette asked. She lifted her hands, uncertain how to demonstrate just how small and unthreatening she was.

"By your bond with Tristan," Uche said. He reached for a piece of the pan bread and broke it into pieces before dunking one in the broth of his stew.

"Lafayette and I just met," Tristan said, but slowly. As if he knew there was something he wasn't quite grasping in his mentor's words.

"True," Uche said between bites of broth-soaked pan bread. "But he can already tell she fills a void for you."

"I fill a void?" Lafayette asked, not sure if the old man was making some sort of joke or not.

"Dieter is clever. He is smart," Uche said. "But he isn't educated. He doesn't have the same background knowledge as Tristan about the things Tristan is most interested in, and he knows it."

"Dieter feels threatened because he finds books boring?" Tristan asked with a puzzled frown. "I mean, he's always keen to listen when I start talking about what I've been reading. He seems like he's interested."

Uche just shrugged.

"But you've known Tristan longer than I have," Lafayette said to Uche. "And you know way more history than I do. And Tristan and I have barely talked together, but you talk to him all the time."

Uche said nothing, his attention apparently fixed on his meal.

"She's right," Tristan said. "Dieter has never been threatened by me coming here. He isn't wildly enthusiastic about me telling him what you and I talk about together in great detail, but he's never said a cross word about you."

Uche still said nothing. But he did pointedly look at their bowls.

Lafayette focused on eating, which wasn't hard to do. After so many days of whatever she could scrape together for food, eating like she used to back when her mother was still alive was still an experience to be treasured.

But she kept sneaking looks at Tristan, trying to figure out what Uche wasn't quite saying. And while Tristan was mostly looking down at his own food, she caught him more than once looking up at her with the same questioning wonder.

"You are behind, Mr. Carey, after taking last night off," Uche said as he stood up to clear the table.

"Right," Tristan said. "And I didn't even think to bring my book bag."

"Didn't you?" Uche said, so dryly Lafayette couldn't tell if he was joking or annoyed or what.

She was starting to realize she didn't get Uche's tone on a lot of occasions. He was an enigma.

"Sorry," Tristan mumbled.

But Uche just gave a dismissive wave before moving the soup pot to the washbasin and filling it with hot water. "No matter. Not studying for you tonight then, but cross-referencing some details for my own project."

"Right," Tristan said. But too brightly. Lafayette didn't quite hold back her smile. *Him,* she could read well enough. He wasn't about to argue, especially as he couldn't claim to really need to study when he hadn't even brought the books to study from.

But she knew without him having to say so that cross-referencing details—whatever that meant—was not a task he particularly liked doing.

She was pulled out of her thoughts with a jump as Uche dropped a stack of books on the table in front of her.

"These are for you," he said even as he turned back to his sink full of dishes.

"For me?" Lafayette asked, hardly daring to touch the books in front of her. They looked old, so old that handling them might prove damaging.

"While you were out, Kora and I assembled a lesson plan for you," Uche said as he washed the bowls, rinsed them under the faucet, then dried them by hand with a shockingly white towel.

"Is that right?" Lafayette asked Kora, who was sitting at her feet.

"I know we came here to help your father, and that is still our primary objective," Kora said in her most Sameera-like voice. "But while we are here, it is a lovely opportunity for you to see what life here at the university could be like for you."

"Oh, definitely," Tristan said with sudden enthusiasm.

"Aren't I a little… young?" Lafayette finished lamely.

Because the minute she was about to say it out loud, she realized the last thing she wanted to do was confess to Tristan that she had never actually been formally schooled. There had been a school in her village, but her mother had considered it far too rudimentary for Lafayette. So she had undertaken Lafayette's education herself.

Which, from what she understood about university life, was going to be a significant obstacle in any plans to be a student there.

Not that she'd ever given that any real thought. She had been focused on her father.

Mostly.

Almost entirely.

And not just because she was pretty sure she was right, that the university wouldn't want her.

"You're old enough to take the entrance exams, but those are eight months away," Uche told her as he dried his hands on the towel before hanging it from a bar over the basin. "Still, that's plenty of time for Kora and I to get you not just up to speed, but likely well ahead of many of your potential classmates."

"History might be hard for her to get into," Tristan said, then flushed like he hated himself for even saying those words.

"Because I don't have any connections?" Lafayette guessed.

"And your parents were expelled," Tristan said.

"They left the school before they could be expelled," Uche corrected him. "Not that the distinction matters to the administration here."

"I'm not sure your advocacy of her will be helpful either," Tristan said, and flushed even more deeply scarlet.

"Perhaps not," Uche said amiably. "But I've been careful to behave over the last few years. The trip south was perhaps inadvisable, but not avoidable. It's increased their suspicion of me. But if I go back to my careful behavior, by the time Lafayette is ready to apply for examination, I should have my reputation quite restored."

"What does that mean?" Lafayette asked. "'Careful behavior'?"

"The project Tristan is assisting me with is a history of Central Planning itself," Uche said. "A heroic telling, of only the approved bits. Thoroughly researched, of course, with all of my best writing. But the farthest thing from controversial."

Lafayette nodded as if she understood that. But mainly she was thinking she knew a little more now about why Tristan was so entirely unthrilled by the work he would be doing this night.

"The curriculum we've designed for you is the widest possible course of study," Kora put in. "You don't have to choose history just because it's what your father did."

"Or what I do," Uche added. "Tristan is my protégé in that. Your options are as open as you can wish them to be."

"Right," Lafayette said, and looked at the books stacked in front of her.

The book on the very top was an encyclopedia of medicinal plants. Like the sort of things her mother had taught her, although this tome was so thick and heavy it just had to contain millions of things she didn't know yet.

It would be fun to dig into. Thoroughly engrossing. Definitely just what she needed to break her almost physical longing to have her parents' journals back where she could see them.

But it was also a distraction. And that worried her.

"We're still going to find a way to help your dad," Tristan said to her. So apparently her thoughts were written all over her face.

She just nodded, not trusting herself to speak.

But everything was getting so complicated.

Worse, she was starting to see where Dieter was coming from about moving slowly and cautiously. Because anything related to helping her father was exactly the sort of things Uche needed to be avoiding. To protect his reputation from further harm.

And as much as she wanted to tell herself that the worry in her mind was about Uche, the fact that she was starting to see what else life in the capital city might have to offer her was a temptation. One she was ashamed to admit even to herself she was finding very, very tempting indeed.

CHAPTER 13

Lafayette slept the next day until midmorning. But after being up until far past midnight just paging through that stack of books, she needed the rest.

She had turned the pages, glanced at the headings and examined the illustrations, but she hadn't done anything like what she'd call proper studying. She had wanted to get a sense of what order she wanted to tackle things in, and she couldn't do that without seeing what there was to study first.

Besides the encyclopedia of medicinal plants, there was also a book on astronomy, another on the principles of physics, and even a very interesting one about the evolution of various animals.

The textbook writers had come up with some very eyebrow-raising theories to explain what Lafayette had understood since she was a small child. The animal world around her, like the plants as well, was a combination of things that had evolved on this planet and things that her ancestors had brought with them from some other, different world.

Not that the textbook writers could ever say that. They might know it. If they didn't, they almost definitely had to suspect it. But Central Planning would ban any book that straight-out said so.

It had been a pleasant night, working her way through all those books while Tristan sat across from her, deep in his own work. The sense of overlapping common purpose unspoken between them was a strange new thing to her.

She supposed her parents had felt this way, her father deep in his historical and archaeological research while her mother was studying plants and medicine.

Maybe everyone at the university felt that way. But to Lafayette, it was special.

And, from the way Tristan glanced up at her from time to time as if just nonverbally checking in, she kind of thought he felt it was special, too.

But now she had another long day to get through, waiting for sunset when Tristan would return. She was a little bit jealous of whatever he must be doing right now. Sitting in classes learning things with other equally driven students. Studying in the library. Even eating and chatting with other students.

Not that Uche was bad company. But outside of mealtimes, he tended to be absorbed in his own work. And he did that work at the desk up in his room, leaving Lafayette to her own devices to pass the time.

She looked over the books he had given her one more time, then decided that as the physics one had struck her as the least initially interesting, she would start with that one. Partly she liked the idea of saving the others as a treat, but partly she was sure that, as a topic she had delved less into than the others, it was one that was bound to have more to teach her.

Also, it was the slimmest of the books. Although, as she settled in with her journal close at hand, she quickly realized that size was deceptive. The text was very dense, and she had to read things over more than once before she quite understood it.

But once she grasped a concept and translated it into her own words for her journal, she knew she could safely turn the page and carry on. She only needed to be taught something once. That had always been true.

She did more reading than writing that day, a fact she was grateful for, as her hand was still a little cramped from the day before. She also stopped when Uche came downstairs, determined to help out with dinner and not keep ducking out on household chores.

Right away, it became clear that help wasn't something he was looking for. In particular, Uche was very proprietary about anything that happened on his cooktop. But he did set her up at the worktable with a knife and a stack of freshly washed potatoes. She peeled them, carefully cutting away the eyes, and diced them up into a bowl while the welcome smell of bacon filled the air.

Lafayette had never seen such thick slices of bacon before. Uche had diced them up as well and was cooking the diced bits in his soup pot. Lafayette could only imagine the flavor they would infuse the potatoes with once they were all added together.

Clearly, this was going to be the best potato soup she'd ever had.

She had just finished dicing the last potato and was handing the bowl to Uche when there was a knock at the door. She turned with a smile to see Tristan ducking inside. She just managed to keep the smile up as she saw Dieter slipping in behind him.

No fancy red shirt today. Just black pants, black shoes, and a black sleeveless shirt. Not that he needed dark colors to disappear into shadows.

"Four of us?" Uche asked without turning around. He was sliding the contents of the potato bowl into the soup pot with one hand while stirring with the other, but apparently he had eyes in the back of his head since Dieter had not made a single sound coming inside.

"Four," Tristan confirmed as he set a bulging book bag next to the door. "It's still light out yet. Do you mind if we go up on the roof and show Lafayette the view of the city?"

"Not at all," Uche said.

Lafayette told herself she was only imagining it, the sense of relief in Uche's words. Like he was grateful for an excuse to get her out of his kitchen.

Tristan and Dieter were already clambering up the spiral stairs, so Lafayette made quick work of washing the bits of potato off of her hands before running up after them.

There was a hatch she hadn't noticed before, just over the wash-basin in the corner of her part of the room. There wasn't any kind of ladder to get up through that hatch, but Dieter just leapt up into the air, higher than Lafayette would've thought possible. He caught the edges with his fingertips, then pulled himself up and out of sight.

"What just happened?" Lafayette said to Tristan, who laughed.

"Dieter grew up on the streets," Tristan said, as if that explained it. But at her blank look, he laughed again. "He kept himself fed by stealing things, then running away. He can climb up onto anything, slip through any kind of hole, and just disappear. I can't explain it. But that little demonstration is the least he can do."

"And you?" Lafayette asked.

"The basin is quite sturdy. It makes a fine step," Tristan said. But rather than climbing up after Dieter, he gestured for Lafayette to go first.

She wasn't so bad at climbing herself, although she was more used to climbing on cliffs of rock or up the sides of crashed ships than she was furniture in a house. Still, once she was up on the lip of the basin with her hand braced against the wall for balance, she could see how a smaller hop from there would bring her up through the hatch.

She jumped, high enough to catch the edge of the hatch with her elbows. Then she kicked out, creating enough momentum to get her belly over the side. From there, it was easy enough to just roll out of the hole and lay on the rough surface of the roof tiles, staring up into the twilit sky.

And at Dieter, smirking down at her.

"I could've helped," he said.

"I didn't need it," she told him as she sat up.

"Clearly," he said. Then he turned to lend a hand to Tristan. Who, despite being several centimeters taller than Lafayette, was struggling to convert grasping the edge with his hands to getting up and over.

Dieter grabbed a fistful of the back of Tristan's tunic and hauled him out of the hole. Lafayette could see a ripple of moving muscle in Dieter's bare arm as he did this. As much as he looked like a skinny street kid, he was clearly all wiry muscle. Someone would dismiss him at a glance to their own peril.

"What are we here to see?" Lafayette asked as she stood up and looked around.

The lights she had seen in the sky before she'd reached the city had looked lovely, in all their shades of blue and pink. But now that she was standing among them, it was downright magical. She could see a defined ring of bright spots of bluish-white light, globes of white equally spaced all around the wall that enclosed the city.

But within that ring, chaos reigned. Some patches were very bright indeed, like around the university buildings just downhill from Uche's house. But other areas were darker, the lights more orange or yellowish, barely illuminating anything around them.

And in the center of it all was that tall building like a spire, with the miniature version of a city on top of it. It looked even higher in the sky now than it had when she'd first seen it. Lafayette wasn't sure if that was a trick of the light, or because she was closer to its base now than she had been before.

The city on top of it particularly intrigued her. It looked so far away. So remote from the rest of everything. She could see the lights of trams criss-crossing the rest of the city, but none of those cable lines ran to that spire, let alone to the city above.

It was at the heart of everything in the city, and yet curiously separate from it.

"We came up here to protect Uche," Tristan told her. "I mean, he knows we're helping you. There's no getting around that. But the more we can keep him out of the specifics, the better."

"He's not exactly spry," Dieter said. "And he's always being watched when he leaves his house. There are real limits to how much he can help."

"I'm not arguing," Lafayette said. "I want to keep him safe as much as I can, too."

"There's the added wrinkle that what we need to do is not exactly illegal, but definitely not anything that Central Planning is going to like us doing," Tristan said.

"I guessed I had already assumed that would be true," Lafayette said. "Just tell me, you know where to start with helping my dad?"

"I know where to start," Dieter said with a grin that actually creeped Lafayette out a bit. There was just too much of a trouble-making edge to it.

Tristan shot her a glance that practically screamed at her that this was Dieter's normal face and it didn't mean anything.

"Where?" Lafayette asked, folding her arms and waiting for Dieter to impress her.

"I know where to find a tablet like the one you have schematics of," he said, then leaned back like he was waiting for her to bathe him in praise.

Which was not her response at all. "Excuse me? Schematics?"

"In the journals," he said with a careless shrug.

"The journals that are locked up hidey-hole in the back of the storage room under the cafeteria?" she asked. 'The ones you told me over and over again you had no interest in reading?"

"The same," he said.

Tristan made a low groaning noise, but they both ignored him.

"The hidey-hole only I have a key to?" Lafayette asked.

Dieter's grin just widened.

"Right," Lafayette said. "No one ever said that was the only key. Got it. So you let yourself in after you told me everything was perfectly safe, and you just helped yourself to the contents?"

"I perused the notebooks for clues," he said. "Everything is still there. Completely secret. And perfectly safe."

"You know where to find a tablet," Tristan said in an attempt to redirect the conversation.

"I've seen one," Dieter said. "And I went to check. It's still where I saw it last. It's not exactly hidden, but I suspect if Central Planning knew where it was, they would've removed it already. I mean, where I found it is in a highly restricted area. But it's still a highly restricted area they've long since stripped of everything else of interest. It's watched, but maybe not closely."

"And where is this highly restricted area?" Lafayette asked.

"I'll keep that to myself for now," Dieter said.

"You still don't trust me?" Lafayette asked, incredulous. "After pawing through my things, *you* don't trust *me*?"

Dieter just shrugged. He never stopped grinning, though.

"Why don't you just bring the tablet to us?" Tristan asked. "Maybe not here at Uche's house. But my room. Or your… place."

"I'm not moving that tablet," Dieter said, his grin gone now. He was deadly serious. "I'll bring you to it so you can glean what you can from it. But no one will be taking it from where it is now. I'm not totally confident that Central Planning *doesn't* know it's there."

"You think it's bait?" Lafayette asked.

"Probably not," Dieter said. "Look, nothing is a hundred percent. I'm weighing the risks. What I'm willing to risk is sneaking you in and out again. What I'm not willing to risk is changing anything about the place I'll be taking you in and out of."

"Getting three of us in and out of a restricted area sounds way riskier than just stealing something," Tristan said. "You steal stuff all the time."

"And yet," Dieter said, giving his friend a look that Lafayette couldn't read at all, "I'm the one weighing the risks. My decision stands."

"Fine," Lafayette said, quickly in case Tristan wanted to argue some more. "Whatever you think. I just want to see this tablet. Does it still function?"

Now Dieter was grinning at her again. "I guess we'll find out."

"We could be risking everything for something that doesn't even work?" Tristan asked.

Dieter shrugged.

"It works," Lafayette said. "He's just winding you up."

"Am I?" Dieter said. But in a way that made her completely unsure. She couldn't read him at all.

Tristan, on the other hand? His growing anxiety was coming off of him in waves. And not just about the sneaking around they were planning to do, or the potential theft they had kind of taken off the table. Lafayette would make no promises on that score.

But no. His anxiety was, if anything, more focused on Dieter and Lafayette.

He just wanted his friends to be friends.

And it kind of stabbed at Lafayette's heart, that most human of wishes. Maybe she could cut Dieter a little slack.

Maybe. He *had* helped himself to her things without telling her, after all.

"Fine," she said at last, and looked up at Dieter. "When do we leave? After dinner?"

"Oh, not tonight," he said, as if that idea was the silliest thing he'd ever heard.

"Not tonight," Lafayette repeated with a weary sigh.

"No, this sort of thing takes planning," Dieter said.

"Weren't you just there?" Tristan said. "You said you know it's still there. So you must've just seen it."

"Me sneaking in and out is one thing," Dieter said. "I'm a very sneaky guy. But three of us? One of us an unknown quantity, and another a known liability when it comes to being sneaky? No offense."

Lafayette thought at first he was referring to her leaving a trail of her father's rare things along the caravan road. But then Tristan mumbled a quiet, "None taken," and she knew there was a story there. Something from their shared childhood.

But from the desperate look Tristan shot her way, she knew he didn't want to get into it.

And from the wide grin on Dieter's face, that troublemaking look he had, she knew it was a story that Dieter would absolutely relish telling.

So there was no way she was going to ask to hear more.

"So I guess you're off again, then?" she said instead. "Planning and arranging. So much work."

"Oh, sure," Dieter said. "But Uche was making bacon and potato soup. So I think I can wait twenty minutes or so before I start planning and arranging."

"You're welcome to stay," Tristan said, then shot Lafayette a nervous look.

"Uche already said it was dinner for four," Lafayette said. As close as she could make herself get to telling Dieter he was welcome.

Although she felt just a little less grudging about extending even that much of an invitation when Tristan gave her a smile of grateful relief.

It was weird how warm she felt just being on the receiving end of that smile.

CHAPTER 14

The bacon and potato soup had not disappointed.

And neither had watching Dieter go out the door soon afterwards.

At Lafayette's refusal to take no for an answer, Uche had finally given in and gone upstairs to his own work, leaving Tristan and Lafayette to do all the dishes and clean up the kitchen before settling down with their own books.

But the principles of physics weren't calling to Lafayette at just that moment.

And Tristan seemed equally uninspired with his own studies. Although he made a few vague noises about just how very far behind he was and how much he should be working hard to catch up.

It had only taken the merest hint of an interest from Lafayette to get him talking about what he knew about history so far.

"Now, remember. I haven't even been accepted to the program yet. I'm not officially a history student, just an aspirant hoping to win a place in that college," he said.

"Yeah, but," Lafayette said, and pointed a finger up to the ceiling, to the rough position of Uche upstairs.

"Right," Tristan said with a chagrined smile. "He says otherwise. But weigh that how you will."

Lafayette held out her hands like she was comparing two imaginary weights. Then she just gave him a smile without telling which hand she had decided held more weight. "Go on."

"You probably know more about this stuff than I do," he said.

"That's just it. I know my dad's version of things. I want to hear yours. I won't interrupt. I'm curious," she said. Then she leaned forward, hands folded, projecting that interested curiosity with every bit of her body language.

"Right," Tristan said, and licked his lips nervously.

Then he talked for three hours straight, almost without break. Not that Lafayette objected. Quite the contrary, she found it all very interesting.

Her father's version of the past had been very much grounded in his archaeological work. Everything he had ever told her had been about which artifact he found at what location, and what he theorized it must have meant.

She knew now that five ships had come to their planet all those years ago. And she'd been on board one of them herself weeks before.

But all her father had known before he found that ship was that an exodus of people far back in the past had moved across the southern grasslands. They had left things behind. It had taken him years to work out where they might have started and where they might have gone. He considered the end point a now-abandoned village east of where Lafayette had grown up. But he had always stressed that was a guess he couldn't back up at all.

But for where he thought it started? Well, he had been very right about that. He had found the ship. And on that ship there had been records of an emergency landing that had been barely controlled, almost a crash. Then the crew and all the people aboard the ship had packed up what they could and walked away.

He had no theory as to why. He hadn't even attempted to come up with one. Because, without an artifact to back it up, he never came up with theories.

Tristan, on the other hand, had no artifacts. He had seen a few things that were stored in the history department vaults, and others that were kept in display cabinets inside the university library. But none of them had been as intriguing as anything her father had found. And he had never been allowed to touch any of them.

What he did have were stories. Old accounts in books, mostly written versions of things people had shared from oral traditions for generations. There was no way to know now how many times those stories had changed before they'd been written down. Although they had continued changing from written account to written account in the ages since.

But Lafayette could guess at what a few things he knew referred to. There were other stories about other traveling groups of early ancestors, which made sense. Five ships had come down. And it made sense that it had taken them time to find each other. A lot of the early stories were about those long walks and desperate searches.

And constructs came up quite a bit. They were treated like ancestral ghosts, but over time, fewer and fewer of them responded.

Lafayette was sure that stories about the ancestral ghosts fading away were far more likely stories of constructs whose power sources finally dwindled down to nothing.

"A lot of things actually make sense, if there was an oral tradition before there was writing again," Lafayette said.

"Why do you say that?" Tristan asked.

"Well, the writing we use, it's not remotely like the writing I learned to read on the ship," Lafayette said. "The language is related. Speaking with Kora when she's Sameera is like trying to speak a very old dialect of the oldest version of our language."

"Ugh," Tristan said with a wince. "I have to take three more years of Old Language courses, and I hate it."

"It's not so bad once you get an ear for it," Lafayette said. "But the written language, it's not even related. All the symbols are different, and they don't track one to one."

"I should probably wait until I have a better grasp of the spoken language first, but I'd love to learn how to read that," he said. "There are objects inside the library locked cases that must be in that language you're talking about. I'd love to know what they say. No one knows."

"Kora and I can teach you," Lafayette said.

"And in the meantime, I can bring you with me into the library," he said. "I'm really curious about those artifacts, what the writing on them says. No one knows, you know. No one can read them."

"I'd love to see them," Lafayette said.

But his schedule over the next few days was packed. Largely because he was spending so much of his off hour time helping Lafayette, so she could scarcely press him to give her more of that. He didn't say so, but she got the sense that his classwork and assistant work together made for a lot more of a load than most of the laughing, chatting students who wandered the university grounds were dealing with.

So Lafayette woke in the morning to the prospect of another long day alone with her books. Although she had just settled down at the worktable with the physics book when Kora whispered, "Someone is coming."

"Tristan?" Lafayette asked. "Or Dieter?"

"No, someone else," Kora said. Then she retreated, like she wasn't sure if she should hide or not.

Lafayette looked down at the stack of books in front of her. Were these something she should hide? But no. If these had been dangerous texts, Uche would have warned her. She'd be following the same protocol as looking at her parents' journals. He wouldn't have set her up in plain view of the front door and left her there during daylight hours to fend for herself.

Her first hint that Kora was right and it wasn't Tristan at the door was when whoever it was knocked and then waited without just opening the door. After the second knock, Lafayette got up from her stool and crossed the room to open the door.

"There you are!" Margo said with her sunny smile. "I brought you something."

"For Uche?" Lafayette asked as she stepped back to let Margo into the house.

"No, silly! For you!" she said.

Then Lafayette saw what Margo had slung over her shoulder. It wasn't a book bag today. It was an immense cloth bag, like the kind they used in her home village to haul laundry to and from the communal laundry building.

Margo set the bag down in the middle of the floor with an oof of effort, although the bag looked more bulky than heavy.

"What's that?" Lafayette asked.

"Open it," Margo said as she slumped onto one of the stools to watch.

Lafayette loosened the strings, then reached inside. She felt layer after layer of clothing packed tightly inside. She grabbed what was on top and shook it out.

It was a dress, all in yellow with little red flowers all over it. It had a full skirt and puffy sleeves.

"What's this for?" Lafayette asked.

"For wearing," Margo said with a laugh. "Look, when you came into town, it was clear the clothes you were wearing had seen better days. And what you're wearing now is in decent shape, but I think it fit you better a growth spurt or two ago. Plus, you've been wearing the same thing for days now. So I made some calls and found you some other options."

"These are all for me?" Lafayette asked, peeking into the bag again.

"Lots of people have stuff they never wear," Margo said. "Some of it is probably not your style, but I got you as many options as I could find. Shoes, too, but they're on the bottom. Not to brag, but I have a good eye. It should all fit you. But just to be sure, don't you want to try stuff on?"

Lafayette glanced over at her physics textbook.

Then she looked at the dress she was still clutching in her hands. It looked so much like one her mother used to wear years ago when Lafayette was small.

"Absolutely," Lafayette said.

Margo helped her get the bulky bag up the tight confines of the spiral staircase. Then Kora came trotting up behind to join Margo on Lafayette's bed as Lafayette pulled off her one good set of clothes and pulled on the dress.

She couldn't imagine where she'd ever wear the thing. It was so fancy, and not at all suitable for climbing onto rooftops or even going on walks with her dog.

But when Margo insisted, she gave a quick spin. And the way the skirt flared out, then wrapped around her legs like a silky hug, she had to admit she'd look for any excuse to wear this dress again.

Luckily, the deeper confines of the bag had more practical things. And it would be downright ungrateful not to try everything out at least once before deciding it wasn't for her.

But her first outfit wasn't hard to pick out at all. The black pants fit snugly, but stretched with all her movements. And they had several cleverly located pockets that let her store things without looking bulky. Especially when she wore the matching vest, which hung loosely to a point just past her hips, but also contained three pockets hidden in its inner folds.

"You really like pockets," Margo said with a laugh.

"I like carrying stuff," Lafayette said with a shrug. "Mostly, I have my trusty satchel over there, but sometimes I have to leave it behind."

"Of course, once you start classes, they'll give you uniforms. Which is nice at first, not having to think about what you're going to wear. And then you get sick of wearing the same thing every day," Margo said, looking down at her own blue outfit with a wrinkle of her nose. "I'm not a fan of blue."

"Once I start classes," Lafayette said almost wonderingly.

"Well, I assumed that's why you were here with Professor Okafo. So you could enroll at the university," Margo said. She gave her a questioning look, like if there were some other reason for Lafayette to be there, it would be impolite to just ask. But like she was dying to know what it could be.

"I have to do a lot of studying before I can even think about that," Lafayette said.

"Yeah, I saw the books downstairs," Margo said. "It looks like you've already made a solid start. You'll catch up in no time. And I know you have Professor Okafo to help you out with anything, but if you'd ever like another tutor closer to your age to explain things to you, I can help."

"You tutor too?" Lafayette asked.

"I *could*," Margo said with another laugh. "But I was thinking more I'd find someone knowledgeable in what you needed help in. I match people up. Like finding outfits no one wears for the girl who needs them."

"Thanks," Lafayette said. "Really, thank you so much."

But Margo just waved it off. "Don't mention it. It's what I do. But think about the tutoring. It might really be helpful for you. Professor Okafo is absolutely your best resource for history, but for other topics? Well, like I said. I can find upper-level students who can explain even the most complicated stuff to you in a way you'll get it just like that."

She punctuated that "that" with a snap of her fingers.

"My father was a historian too," Lafayette said. She didn't want to explain the caveats on that, of how he had either been expelled or left before he could be expelled or whatever the actual circumstances had been.

And she also more than half assumed that Margo already knew all that, anyway. It seemed like everyone did. Even though it had been almost twenty years ago.

"It's a tough career path," Margo said. Her bright sunniness was muted now, and she spoke in a low, somber tone. "There's good work to be done still, of course. But it is not the field our brightest minds are flocking to."

Lafayette said nothing. Which Margo apparently interpreted to mean something Lafayette wasn't even thinking, as she rushed to add, "Not that Tristan Carey isn't a bright mind. Quite the contrary. But he's also stubborn enough to succeed where others not only fail, but don't even have the courage to try. Let's call him the exception that proves the rule."

"I wasn't thinking of Tristan," Lafayette admitted.

"Oh. Well, I was," Margo said. Then she blushed. "I do that a lot. But never mind. All I'm saying is, if you have interests outside of history but you're feeling overwhelmed by the challenges of pursuing an academic path that the two people you're closest to can't exactly help you with... well, again, I'm your girl."

"My mother studied botany," Lafayette said. "Medicinal plants, mostly."

"That would be very cool," Margo said. "That's the sort of thing you can get a grant to do fieldwork in."

"I don't know what that means," Lafayette said.

"It means you tell Central Planning what you're curious about, and they send you with everything you need wherever you need to go to study and learn more," Margo said. "They don't give grants for history anymore, but something that helps all of us? Like finding new medicines? You could see the whole known world, studying that."

"That does sound tempting," Lafayette said.

Which, if she was being honest with herself, *did* sound tempting. After living in just one place for her whole life, if her months of travel had taught her anything, it was that travel was something she felt called to do more of.

She guessed she had inherited her father's wanderlust. Or, at least, his quest for answers that couldn't be found close to home.

Which was ironic. Both in that she had often hated the fact that he was always away, finding those answers, all throughout her childhood.

But also because the one thing she wanted more than anything was to bring him home again. She couldn't entertain thoughts of traveling herself. Not now. Not until he was safe.

But after?

After would have to wait to be thought about until it *was* after, Lafayette told herself with a sigh.

Then she had a thought she really hadn't seen coming.

She found herself hoping she'd see Dieter again, and sooner rather than later.

CHAPTER 15

ristan was there on time for dinner, the book bag over his shoulder as overly stuffed as the day before. But when Lafayette shot him a questioning look, he just shrugged.

So he didn't know where Dieter was, or if he was coming, or what was going on.

Uche had prepared a roasted chicken with root vegetables and dark, meaty mushrooms in a rich sauce that was like nothing Lafayette had ever tasted before. He more readily agreed to let Lafayette do the cleaning up than he had the night before. She hoped that meant he thought she had done a good job.

But it was probably because he wanted the time to lecture Tristan about how far behind he was with his coursework. He was keeping up in his classes, and just barely keeping up with the assistant tasks he did for Uche officially.

But he was behind in the studying he was meant to be doing in history. And Lafayette knew that was largely because she'd taken up all his time the night before. She felt a little bit guilty about that.

And a lot curious how Tristan was keeping up with everything else Uche had just listed out that he was doing. She had been beat when he'd left the night before, but all she had had to do was stumble up the stairs and into bed. He still had to walk back to his room, and then it sounded like he'd hit the books before sleeping, then gotten up even earlier than she had to make his first class.

Yeah, she was feeling a lot guilty.

It didn't help that the minute Uche had gone back up to his own desk, she and Tristan both heard a soft sound at the door. Not a knock, more a gentle grazing of fingernails on the wood. But they both knew what it meant.

Dieter was there. It was time.

"Kora, I need you to stay here with Uche, okay?" Lafayette said as she dropped to one knee and put her hands on the dog's furry face.

"I can keep watch," Kora agreed. "You'll be safe?"

"Yes. It might be longer than last time, though. Are you going to be okay with that?" Lafayette asked.

"I'll keep a better sense of time," Kora said in her more Sameera sounding voice. Like the construct was working to dominate the doggy nature a little more strongly, if only for a moment.

"Good. If Uche asks, tell him not to worry," Lafayette said.

"He won't ask," Tristan said to her in a low voice as he opened the door. "He can't. But he knows what's going on."

Lafayette shot a look at the ceiling, imagining Uche at his desk upstairs. She could see him, pen poised but still, listening to them moving around downstairs.

Yeah, he knew what they were up to. But he didn't want to *know* know. They had to leave him the ability to say he had no idea where they went or what they were up to.

In case they got caught. And people from Central Planning came here with questions.

"I hope this works," Lafayette hissed at Dieter, a bit more accusingly than she had meant to. "It's a risk. It better pan out."

"No promises," Dieter said.

But Tristan said, "Dieter doesn't take risks that don't pan out," in the exact same moment.

Dieter gave him an annoyed look, but Tristan just shrugged, unbothered.

Lafayette touched the pockets of her new pants, checking the contents as Tristan closed the door behind them. She had the key on its ring, in case she needed it. And she had her father's multitool. That might come in handy. But after going through the contents of her satchel several times that afternoon after Margo had left, she hadn't found a single other thing she owned that had any possible use on this mission.

Not that she knew what they were about to do in anything but the sketchiest of details.

Dieter waved for them to follow, and Lafayette fell into step beside Tristan, trailing behind Dieter as he slipped from shadow to shadow. He stopped several times, she supposed to listen although for all the world it looked like he was scenting the air the way Kora would do.

She had been holding on to a secret hope that wherever they were going, it would mean going by tram. She longed to see what the inside of those cable-riding wagons looked like. And she wanted to see the view as they glided all but silently over the lights of the city.

Alas, he was taking them into a neighborhood that was louder than Uche's, but darker. Which was unnerving. She could hear people carousing, children shrieking in bedtime rebellions, and dogs barking. And she couldn't see a bit of it.

She was peering into the darkness so intently in the hopes of catching a glimpse of anything that she didn't realize Dieter had stopped until she had collided with his back.

His hard-muscled back. His entire appearance was such a lie. He was nothing like the undernourished former waif he clearly wanted to be perceived as.

"This way," he hissed at her. Which, in the darkness, wasn't helpful. But then his hands were on her elbows, guiding her towards something. Something set in the ground.

They were going down through an open hatch in the middle of the street. Her feet found metal rungs, and then her hands found them too. The rungs were cold, wet, and covered with something both gritty—which she could deal with—and slimy, which she liked far less.

She was going to get dirty, wherever they were going. That was clear.

And in her new clothes, too.

It was a short climb that ended in nothing but open air. Lafayette bit back a yelp of alarm, clutching the rungs far more closely to her body than she really wanted to. But suddenly having nothing under her feet was, to put it mildly, startling.

"It's only a meter or two," Dieter told her. It was hard to tell in the darkness, but it sounded like he was laughing at her. "Just drop down."

"Tell me why I had to go first?" she shot back.

But she let go and dropped. It was, indeed, more like one meter than two, and she landed easily.

But she landed in a puddle of water that soaked her up to her ankles. And the water was cold and slimy, just like the rungs had been.

She took a few steps back to leave some room for the others, but Dieter didn't land where she did. He swung his legs and angled his body to land as gracefully as any cat on the far end of that puddle where the concrete ground was quite dry.

"You could've told me that," she grumbled as they both watched Tristan's feet come down towards them.

"I could've," Dieter agreed, a little too merrily.

Then he stepped back so that Tristan could attempt to mimic his move. It was less graceful, but successful enough. Only Lafayette was stuck with shoes that were drenched, the soles slick with whatever the slime was.

"Head towards the light," Dieter said.

"Why don't you take the lead?" Lafayette offered.

"Because I'm guarding our rear," he said.

"I'll go," Tristan said, and stepped past Lafayette to lead the way. But she didn't want him tripping over anything in the dark any more than she wanted to herself. So she fell into step beside him.

The light up ahead was dim and distant, and their steps echoed around them as they walked through a slick, stone-walled tunnel. Every so often, they passed under the rungs of another ladder, but there were no side tunnels. No turnings. Nowhere to go but onward, or back.

"Where are we?" Lafayette asked when she couldn't stand the silence any longer.

"Utility tunnels," Dieter said from behind her. "It's hard to see in this light, but there are access panels in the walls here and there. This is how maintenance is done for the utilities that run to all the buildings in the capital city."

"And why is the floor wet?" Lafayette asked. Because her feet were squishing in her shoes with every step.

"It's only wet under the hatches," Dieter said, the hint of a laugh back in his voice. "It runs down when it rains, but the sun never gets down here, so it just sits and gets funky."

"Hence the swinging thing," Tristan said to her.

"Which I would've loved to have known about before," Lafayette said.

"Sorry. I don't come down here much," Tristan said.

"And he does?" she asked, jerking a thumb back over her shoulder towards Dieter.

"He lives down here," Tristan said.

"She doesn't need to know that," Dieter said, annoyed.

"You live down here? In a sewer?" Lafayette asked.

"It's not the sewer," Dieter shot back. But then he added, "It's not all sewer. It's access tunnels. And yes, it's my home. *Our* home."

As if his words had conjured things out of the dark, Lafayette suddenly had that feeling again, of pairs and pairs of unseen eyes, all watching her.

Then the access tunnel widened out into some sort of underground chamber filled with crates. The crates were up on pallets, which made Lafayette think Dieter hadn't been entirely honest about how wet things got down here. Clearly, precautions were being taken to keep things dry.

Then, by some unseen and unheard cue, a dozen globes of light all ignited at once. Lafayette sucked in a breath and threw an arm over her eyes, the sudden intensity of light so jarring it literally hurt to find herself accidentally staring up into it.

Dieter was saying something, but his words were like nothing Lafayette had ever heard before. It wasn't the common language, and it wasn't the older version she had learned on board the ship either. It was something else. Maybe newer. Definitely slangier. It had a vibe to it, a rhythm and flow.

But what it didn't have, at least not for her, was any sort of meaning.

"Don't look up," Dieter said to her, even as he grasped her elbow to guide her. "We're just passing through, but the locals would prefer it if you didn't get all observe-y on the way through."

"What?" Lafayette asked.

"They wanted to blindfold you," he said, as if her question had been some sort of argument or refusal. "Let's just keep moving. They have only claimed this neighborhood. We'll be out of it in ten minutes, tops."

Lafayette just focused on her own soaked feet, watching her step as she walked.

There were more puddles here. And as much as they didn't have a slimy sheen in the lights from above, she still was happier not splashing through any more of them than she could help.

Then, just as suddenly and as without apparent cue as before, all the lights went out again, and they were plunged back into darkness.

Except this time, Dieter clicked on a hand light. It wasn't like the lanterns she had used back in her father's camp. It was smaller than that, barely bigger than his thumb, and emitting only a thin, wavering beam. But it was better than nothing.

They continued on down another tunnel with no turnings or intersections.

"Where are we going?" Lafayette asked, just fighting the urge to ask how far instead.

"Nearly there," Dieter said. He was still holding her elbow, as if she was more of a risk than Tristan, who was walking unassisted on Dieter's other side.

"I've never been this way before," Tristan said. Which Lafayette thought was odd. So far as she could tell, this looked exactly like the last tunnel they had been walking through. And he had been familiar with that. What was he seeing now that was telling him this was different?

"We're quite a bit closer to the center of the city than I've taken you before," Dieter said.

"How close?" Tristan asked.

Dieter said nothing. But the light from his hand light was reflecting off his teeth in a flash as he grinned.

Then the tunnel widened out into another chamber, this one larger than the last. And there were a few random lights here, large globes in metal structures just like the streetlights in the city above. They weren't arranged in a line or a ring or anything, just set amongst what appeared to be the churned up rubble of a cobblestoned road.

"Where are we?" Lafayette asked, straining to see anything in the watery light from those globes.

But Tristan sucked in a breath before saying, "I know where we are. I just don't know why."

"Come on," Dieter said, giving his friend a chuffing blow to the shoulder before putting his now not needed light back into his pocket. "You're looking for a way to talk to that ship up in space, right? And to find where the other four came down?"

"Yeah," Tristan said slowly. But then he cursed under his breath. "Dieter, this rumor has been debunked several times over history."

"Debunked by Central Planning," Dieter said. "Come on. You know better than that. Their vigorous debunking is exactly how you know it's all true, right? Lafayette knows what I mean."

Lafayette did not, in fact, know what he meant.

But then she saw a gleam from up ahead, where the ground was most churned up. Something massive was coming up out of that ground. Or had been thrust down into it. Something violent had happened to all that earth was clear, but the direction was less so.

It had happened long ago, though. Of that, Lafayette was quite sure.

She had seen things like this before. On both a smaller and a larger scale.

"Where are we?" she asked. She wasn't sure why she was whispering.

"You've seen the spire," Dieter said. "They've covered it with a bunch of junk on the exterior, and they put all of their Central Planning buildings right on top of it. But if you've seen what you've told me you've seen, surely you know what this is."

Lafayette looked again at the very spire-like shape of what was ahead of them. They had barely gotten any closer to it, but she made some adjustments in her mind to the scale of the thing they were approaching.

"It can't be. There's no way a ship crashed here and ended perfectly vertical with its back end straight up in the air," Lafayette said. "It's impossible."

"I can walk you around to the far side," Dieter said. "It's a little out of our way, but I can show you the supports that were built there."

"The spire is a ship," Tristan said. He sounded mentally tired. "Central Planning is built on top of a ship. And from there they tell the rest of us the stories of ships bringing us all here from the far side of the universe are all lies."

"Yeah, cheeky of them, isn't it?" Dieter said.

"Supports," Lafayette said. "It crashed, and they jacked it up onto its nose to make a building out of it?"

"A very tall building," Dieter said, as if that were an important point.

Which, yeah. It probably was.

"And we're here because you found a tablet?" Tristan said.

"Yeah, but to get to it, we're going to have to go inside the ship," Dieter said. Then he looked at Lafayette. "Nothing new for you, right?"

"Or you either, apparently," she said.

But Dieter just grinned at her.

CHAPTER 16

ieter led them to a hatch in the side of the ship, not exactly like the one Lafayette had used to get inside the other ship, but similar. This one didn't open onto the endless curving corridor of a ring, for one thing.

It opened part way up a long series of stairways. There were low-level red lights on every landing, enough to see the steps by. But counting those lights was just barely possible, in the sense that while Lafayette could see the lights as distinct dots above and below, they were in both directions so numerous it would take time and attention to do so.

"Up," Dieter said briskly, and started climbing the steps at a steady rate that told Lafayette that however far up they were going, it wasn't going to be a short walk. She knew Dieter well enough by now to know short walks were taken at a run. This, this was the sort of pace she set in the morning knowing she'd be keeping it up all day.

Her shoes were still squishing around her feet, and her socks felt so disgusting she was probably going to throw them away once she'd gotten back home and taken them off. But if there was one thing Lafayette could always be relied on to do, it was putting one foot in front of the other and doing that over and over again for however long it took.

Tristan just trailed along behind the other two, lost in his own thoughts. From the snatches of words he was huffing under his breath, Lafayette gathered he was still trying to work out how the fact that the spire in the center of the city he had spent every day of his life in was actually a ship from space was something he had simultaneously always known and never quite believed.

Lafayette had some sympathy for him. She had seen a ship in a crater. She had seen that same ship taking off with no trees or earth around it to hide its shape at all.

And then she'd seen the spire when she'd entered the city, and she had never thought "ship" at all.

There were a lot of added features that disguised its use, that was true.

But it was also made of metal. And that she *had* noticed. And she had just chalked it up to the difference in things in the city from back home in the village.

It was still mind-boggling, that someone between landfall and now had used some sort of machines to push the ship up on its nose to stand vertical. Why? It must have been a tremendous amount of work.

And what if they had failed at it? It would've fallen over, surely crushing everything in its unpredictable path.

"Oh," she said aloud as another thought struck her.

"What's that?" Tristan asked her from where he was trudging behind her.

"The city walls. That's the edge of the crater. The whole city is sitting in the crater from where this ship fell," she said.

Tristan sighed. "Sure. It seems obvious now."

"People have noticed," Dieter said to them both. "Over and over again. Hence the rumors. And the quashing of the rumors. Then they add a few more details to the exterior to try to disguise things."

"And you know this how?" Lafayette asked.

"The same way I know what happened to all of Uche's students," he said. "Unofficial histories."

"Why aren't we looking at those?" Lafayette asked.

"I'm curious about that myself," Tristan said.

"Because you'd never be able to read it. It's not in the common tongue," Dieter said. "And there's nothing in them about how to bring a ship down. They don't go quite that far back. More's the pity."

Lafayette was a tiny bit jealous of how effortlessly he could speak in long sentences. Even she was starting to get a little bit winded. And their climb was far from over.

It took another hour of walking, broken up by a few short breaks that Tristan had absolutely insisted on, before Dieter finally stopped climbing stairs. They were on another landing, but this one had a hatch on it.

A closed hatch. Lafayette touched what she knew was the control panel beside it, but it did nothing. It was perfectly inert. Only the red lights were still under power, then. Everything else was as apparently dead as it had been on the other ship before her dad had started touching things in engineering.

"I can open it," Dieter said, and took a pry bar out of his back pocket. It was a small one, little bigger than his hand, and once he had it jammed between door and doorjamb, there wasn't much room for him to get any leverage.

But apparently he didn't need any. He just put the flat of his hand against it and leaned in. The door shrieked in metallic protest, then slid back out of the way.

"I had a harder time with mine," Lafayette said as they slipped inside.

"I'm sure you did," Dieter said, putting his pry bar back in his pocket. Then he led the way down the corridor beyond.

The lighting here was still low and red, which made the other colors muted. But even so, Lafayette found this corridor like the rest of this ship: familiar, but subtly different. There was the same worn sort of carpeting beneath their feet as in the other ship, but the pattern here was different. The doors lining the corridor were arranged differently.

But she could still read the signage. And she knew without Dieter telling her that he was taking them to engineering. She could read it on the signs as he navigated the rights and lefts of the turns that took them there.

Only he didn't lead them all the way there. He stopped just short of it, taking out the pry bar to open a smaller door just before the main double doors that were labeled engineering.

The door he was opening said "chief engineer."

"Have you been in there?" Lafayette asked, pointing to the other doors.

"They definitely watch that," Dieter said to her as he leaned into the pry bar to compel the door to open.

Which wasn't a no. But if they could find what they needed in the chief engineer's private quarters, it was the more acceptable risk. So she didn't argue.

The room beyond was so tiny that it was downright crowded with all three of them inside. There was a narrow bed built into the far wall, and beside it a desk that looked like it could be folded back into the wall and stowed away to free up some space.

Lafayette opened a row of drawers and then the doors of a cabinet above them, but there was nothing inside. And the bed had been stripped of bedding. Like the other ship, everything was gone now.

"It's here," Dieter said as he lifted the mattress out of the bed frame. There was a long cut down the bottom edge of the mattress like someone had sliced it open with a knife. Dieter stuck his hand inside and slid out a tablet, which he immediately handed to Lafayette.

It was a thing of beauty. That was her first thought. The tablets she had used before on the other ship had all been school tablets, meant for children's hands, sturdy and built for hard use.

This was delicate, thinner than the width of her pinkie finger, and made from a shiny kind of metal that looked like silvery moonlight. On the back of it was some sort of paper design that had been glued down onto it, an arrangement of ribbons and flowers that looked like it had been drawn in ink by hand then painted. Its colors had faded with time, but even in the reddish light of the single bulb over the door-frame, it looked like it had once been a soft shade of rose.

"Can you use it?" Tristan asked as he peered down at it over her shoulder.

"Yeah," Lafayette said, turning it over in her hands to look at the blank screen. Then she found the switch and flicked it to its other position, holding her breath that something would happen.

The screen flickered to life, and they all released the breath they had been holding. Lafayette shot a brief glance up at Dieter's face, surprised to find him so invested in the moment. But then she turned her attention back to the tablet.

And was disappointed to find she couldn't read a word of it.

It looked for all the world like someone's handwriting. But how anyone could write on a screen, she wasn't sure. She could scroll through it like Sameera had taught her to, but every page she scrolled to was the same.

"It's handwriting," she told the other two as she continued her rather random search of the documents. "I think it's the language I learned, but I don't think this is particularly good handwriting. It's going to take me some time to figure out what character each of these pen strokes is meant to represent."

"We don't have a lot of time," Dieter told her.

"I know," Lafayette sighed. But she sat down on the bunk, anyway. She wanted to rest the tablet on her knees and use both hands.

Then she realized that touching the top of the screen opened up some sort of menu. She had used menus like this on the school tablets. It was how you moved from book to book, as each tablet had contained thousands of books.

The menus were written in clear text, not handwriting, but printed like the signs in the corridors. These she could read.

"This is a personal journal," she told them, pointing at the label across the top of the menu as if that could possibly mean anything to them. But they said nothing, just watched her work. "It's not a study journal. It's more like a diary. I think these markings here that split up the larger chunks of paragraphs are dates."

"They look like dates," Tristan said. "The spacing, you know?"

"Yeah," Lafayette said. But her attention was still on the labels of the menu options.

Then she found one that just said "convert." Convert to what? On a whim, she pressed her fingertip down on that word.

And all the handwriting shimmered, then reformed as printed text.

"Nice," Dieter said.

"You can read this?" Tristan asked her.

"More easily than the handwriting," Lafayette said.

But it was still so much information to get through. And she was afraid to ask Dieter just how much time they had. It was never going to be enough. She knew that for sure.

"If the owner of this tablet was the chief engineer, this should be really useful," Tristan said. "Like really, really useful."

"I told you," Dieter said, but there was a false air to his smugness. He had only hoped the tablet would be of any use to them. He knew he had just gotten lucky. But he was going to take the credit for it, anyway.

"There's a lot on here," Lafayette said as she scrolled through the now clearly labeled entries.

"It's a diary, right?" Dieter said. "So start at the end."

Which made perfect sense. So Lafayette scrolled to the last page and started to read.

"I don't think the conversion was a complete success," she said after several minutes of focused concentration on the words. "Some of the word choices are weird. I think the handwriting was just off. But I can't read that at all, so I guess we'll never know."

"But is there anything useful?" Tristan asked.

"This diary didn't belong to the chief engineer, so I don't know how it ended up in this room," she said. "But it did belong to a woman who was an engineering intern. About our age, I'm guessing. She was really worried because the ships were crashing and then losing contact with each other. She wasn't in charge, though, so she didn't know what was going on."

"So, this ship was the last one to go down?" Tristan asked.

"It sounds that way," Lafayette said. "And I don't think they even crashed. I think when the other four ships were down, this one just set down. This woman, whoever she was, was hoping they would make contact with the other four ships soon. She had family on all of them."

"But if they didn't crash, why didn't she write any more entries after they landed?" Tristan asked.

"A really good question," Lafayette said with a sigh. "I want to go back over the earlier entries. Maybe she has more details there about where the other ships went down."

"How does that help your dad?" Dieter asked.

Which was a fair question. It had been the focus of his life's work, finding those ships. But finding the ships wouldn't help him get down.

"I need more time here," Lafayette said.

"No," Dieter said.

"I need to study this ship to figure out how to get my dad down," she said.

Dieter leaned in closer before saying, "No," a second time.

"Then I need to keep this tablet," she said, folding it against her chest and wrapping both her arms around it. "I need something."

"You're going to take that tablet, and then a week from now, you're going to be demanding I bring you back here anyway," Dieter predicted.

"Probably," she admitted, and raised her chin.

"Can we just stay until we learn everything?" Tristan asked.

"No," Lafayette said with regret. "Kora."

"And Uche," Tristan agreed.

"And your classes," Dieter put in.

They were all silent for a minute. The ship around them was completely soundless. Not even the bulbs emitting the red light made so much as a hum.

Then Dieter gave in with a growl of self-directed anger. "Fine. But keep that thing hidden. I'm not even kidding. Not even Uche can know you have it. It's not just your life on the line here, you know."

"I know," Lafayette said, her heart already soaring at the thought of all the tablet had to teach her.

But Dieter wasn't done. "It's Uche. It's Tristan's entire family. And it's the lives of my entire community. They let you pass through to get here. Don't make me regret talking them into doing that."

"I won't," Lafayette swore. "I promise."

Dieter looked like he wanted to say something cutting about her promises, but in the end, he just nodded.

"Let's go. We've been here too long already," he said.

Lafayette tried not to skip too much as she followed him back to the endless staircase. But she couldn't help feeling a little elated.

This had all worked out so much better than she had hoped. She had a tablet now. She had the key to unlimited knowledge.

There had to be a way to get her dad down safely. And this long-dead engineering intern was going to help her find out how.

CHAPTER 17

The trip back down the stairs felt like it took longer than the trip up had. Lafayette thought this was partly because, with the tablet clutched tightly to her chest, she was starting to get that itchy "someone's watching me" feeling on the back of her neck. Even though she knew the ship wasn't really watching her. The power was off. It wasn't possible for it *to* watch her.

Unless whatever robots it had watching were on the same system as the red lights that guided their way. But she didn't think that was possible. She certainly saw no sign of anything that looked like it could be watching them go by.

But mainly it felt like it took longer because they were moving slower. Or, at least, Tristan was. Dieter's steady strides ate the distance easily, and Lafayette, after the bliss of three days of rest, wasn't working too hard to keep up with him.

But Tristan clearly spent most of his time poring over books and journals, sitting in chairs. The furthest he ever walked was from the library to Uche's house, and that wasn't very far at all. The cafeteria where he ate his daytime meals was on the way.

"Sorry," he mumbled, not for the first time, when Dieter stopped on one of the landings to let him catch up.

"It'll be easier when we're off the stairs," Lafayette said. Although she didn't think that was necessarily true. The wet floors and darkness of the utility tunnels were not much faster to navigate. And she could see he was getting tired. But she had to find something to say to keep him moving. "It's not far. And it's only a little bit of an uphill slope the whole way."

Tristan nodded, but refused to stop where they were waiting for him. He just kept trudging on with his head down, not really noticing when first Dieter and then Lafayette passed him again to take the lead once more.

"We aren't going back the way we came," Dieter told Lafayette.

"Why not?" Lafayette asked. "It felt like the fastest way."

"Oh, it's definitely the shortest line between the two points," Dieter said. Then he nodded his head towards the tablet she held clutched to her chest. "That's not going anywhere near my people. And we're definitely not taking it straight back to Uche's house either. We need to throw in all the misdirection we can."

"You really think they're watching us?" Lafayette asked, looking up at the red light as they passed under it on one of the landings before heading down the next flight of steps. She still saw nothing but featureless wall and that single bare bulb of light.

"If not here, then definitely in the tunnels," Dieter said. "I trust my people better than I trust anyone. But that doesn't mean they're all worthy of that trust. Central Planning gets in everywhere. It's just what they do. Like mold in the walls after the rainy season. You can fight it, but you can never totally win."

"So if we avoid your people, we can avoid the attention of spies, maybe?" Lafayette asked.

"I'm doing all I can here," Dieter said. Then he picked up his pace. Which might do the job of ending the conversation with Lafayette, but was clearly more than Tristan could handle.

Dieter reached the bottom of the stairs and disappeared out through the hatch into the underground chamber that Lafayette still didn't totally understand. But she waited at the bottom of the stairs for Tristan, who had fallen three flights behind, to catch up.

The bottom of the chamber looked like it had once been a level street, covered in cobblestones, like the streets above. Or maybe more than a street, like a wide square plaza all paved in stones.

Only how had the ship ended up piercing through the middle of such a thing? There had been nothing here when it came down, surely? And yet, the cobblestones around the exterior of the ship's hull looked buckled up and blown back. Like there had been a ripple of energy through the ground itself, tearing everything up.

Her best theory was that the ship had sat at more of an angle, like the one her father had found, and they had built a city of sorts around it. Only later, after everything had been paved for some time, had they decided to pull it upright, build the supports and bury them, and turn the crash sight into a spire.

Which must have happened centuries ago, to account for the fact that the current city was quite a way over her head now. They'd built over this impact zone, and then they'd built on top of the ship, and then they'd added all the extra features along the sides to disguise the shape of the ship beneath.

She was suddenly very curious about what Uche Okafo was actually working on. The history of Central Planning. For how many generations had they been working to bury her planet's shared history?

And the question that burned in her mind most strongly of all: why?

"You guys coming?" Dieter called from somewhere off to the south end of the chamber.

"Yeah," Tristan said glumly as he emerged from the hatch beside Lafayette. His face was beet red, and not from embarrassment this time.

"Are you doing okay?" Lafayette asked.

He just nodded, like the one word he had uttered had left him too tapped out for another. He turned in the direction of Dieter's voice, and Lafayette matched his pace. It was slow going, but she refused to leave his side. She didn't want him to fall behind.

Dieter led them down another long, turnless utility tunnel. This one ran far longer than the one they had followed to get to the ship in the first place, gently sloping up and, at Lafayette's best guess, to the south and east end of the city beyond the spire.

Away from Uche's house and the university. About as far away as they could get without leaving the city entirely.

Tristan was barely keeping his feet moving when Dieter finally stopped at the bottom of another ladder. He signaled for Lafayette to wait there with Tristan, and she grabbed Tristan's arm to pull him to a stop as she watched Dieter scramble up that ladder with silent speed.

Tristan was swaying on his feet, eyes half-closed, and Lafayette remembered that in addition to his general lack of conditioning, he had also been getting very little sleep since she'd come to the city. And she didn't get the sense he got enough sleep even on a normal day.

She heard a soft whistle, more a hiss of breath between teeth than a proper sound. But she knew without asking this was Dieter telling them it was safe to come up.

She nudged Tristan, and he shook himself out of his doze. It took two hops for him to catch onto the bottom rung of the ladder over-head, and for an endless minute while she held her breath, it looked like dangling there was the best he could do.

But then he started moving up, grunting as he used just his arms until he was far enough up to get his feet on the bottom rung.

Lafayette stayed where she was, peering up to where she could just make out the diffuse glow of a distant streetlight outlining Dieter's upper half as he reached in to help Tristan get out of the hatch.

Then it was her turn. She felt around the inside of her vest until she found the pocket at the small of her back. It was an awkward location, but it was the pocket that was big enough to hold the tablet so she could use her hands to climb.

She was more than a little paranoid she'd fall on it like she had fallen on the Sameera construct's power supply. But this was a ladder, not a wall of intertwined vines. And it was nowhere near the two hundred meters she had climbed that day.

Also, there were no winged cat beasts chasing her down in a pack this time.

She jumped and caught the bottom rung and climbed as quickly as she could. As much as she wanted to duck away from Dieter's helpful grasp, she didn't want to risk the tablet. At all. Better to let him think she needed the help. Which she absolutely didn't.

Dieter slid the hatch shut behind them as Lafayette blinked in the sudden brightness of the streetlights. They were alternating pink and blue on this street, which was wider and straighter than the streets around the university.

The buildings on either side of the road looked like homes. They weren't fenced in like the homes in the villages around the city. But they also felt separate from each other in a way that they didn't in her home village. Like the plots of land they stood on were distinct to the families and not common ground.

She couldn't see the stars past the light from the city, but she saw one of the two moons far off in the west. It was very late, far past midnight. No wonder Tristan was so tired.

Dieter wiped the grit from the hatch off his hands, then pointed up the street. Lafayette couldn't tell at first why he'd picked that particular direction, but when they reached the darkest point between two of the streetlights, she could just make out the outline of a tower in the sky up ahead.

A tram station. Although nothing was moving along the cables in any direction at the moment.

Lafayette stayed closed to Tristan, but Dieter was all over the place. He'd jog ahead, then fall back, always sliding in and out of shadows she didn't even know were there half the time. At first she thought he was just one of the high energy, impatient, unfocused types she remembered from back home. The kids who couldn't stick to one task no matter how much they tried.

Then she realized he was doing exactly what the patrols around the caravans had done. But where they had had teams of people as well as dogs, Dieter was working on his own. But Lafayette had no doubt it would be all but impossible for anyone to get the jump on them.

Not that anyone was awake in this part of town. It was dead silent.

More than that, she didn't have that feeling of being watched here.

They reached the base of the tower, and Lafayette saw it wasn't so much a solid building as a hollow shell. At ground level, every side of the building was an open arch to allow as many people to move in and out as was possible. And the interior was mostly stairs, although there was a lift in one corner for cargo.

Dieter led the way up four flights of stairs to the waiting platform on top of the tower, just under the dome.

"We'll wait here," he said to her even as Tristan was slumping down into one of many empty benches.

"Until?" Lafayette asked.

"The first tram isn't until just before dawn," he told her. "We'll try to fit in with the morning commuters. We're going to be making some tight connections to throw off any tail we pick up, so rest up now. I need you both sharp when we're on the move."

"I'll be fine," Tristan said. "I just need a minute."

Dieter put a reassuring hand on Tristan's shoulder even as he threw a pointed look Lafayette's way.

Lafayette knew what he was asking of her. He wanted her to watch Tristan. She gave him a silent nod, and he returned it before doing that fading into the shadows thing again.

But she knew wherever he was, he was watching out for trouble. And watching over the two of them.

Lafayette sat down on the bench next to Tristan to wait. Not a minute later, Tristan slumped further down and then up against her, until his head was resting on her shoulder. She didn't mind. But she was far too keyed up to sleep herself.

And there was no one else in the station. It was just a big, echoing space all around them. If anyone did start trickling in to also wait for the first tram of the day, she'd hear their feet on the stairs long before they reached a point where they could see her.

She waited as long as she could bear to. Then she moved slowly, trying to jostle the sleeping Tristan as little as possible, as she pulled the tablet out of the back pocket of her vest.

She sat with her knees drawn up close to her chest. A little tricky as the slime-slicked soles of her shoes wanted to slip away from the bench seat. She pulled the drapey sides of her vest close around her.

And then she turned on the tablet and started touching and tapping her way through the screens again.

She worked her way backwards from the diary entry she had read before. Most of the words she only glanced at, but she was keeping an eye out for any clue of where the other ships had gone.

She was scanning for keywords like "ship" or "crash" or "landing." But what she found was a map.

It was clearly drawn by hand, just as the words on the tablet had originally been written by hand. And it was filled with the mark that she knew denoted a question in the old language. So the woman who had drawn it wasn't sure of the scale or even the locations.

But Lafayette sucked in a breath of amazement, anyway. Because she was pretty sure she was looking at a map of the locations of all five ships. She had found what she had hardly dared to hope to find: a map that linked up all of her father's various maps. A map that put all those other maps into context.

A map she could use to actually find things like the other ships.

She summoned up a mental image of her father's work, a composite version of the various maps she had seen in his journals. The details might be off, and they might even be off in a way that would really matter.

But she knew she was right. In her bones, she knew it. She could put a finger on the ship she had just been standing in a few hours before. In the middle of the Great Grassy Sea.

And she could put another finger on another location, far to the south and west. Where the jungle-filled crater was.

That left three more locations. One was far to the south, past a band of mountains. Another was to the east, but at the bottom of the Watery Sea.

And the last was far to the north. Far, far to the north. But, unlike the other two, there was nothing in the way that couldn't be walked over. It was reachable.

But it was so very far away.

"I've seen that," Tristan said close to her ear. So he was awake again, and looking at the tablet she was hiding in the folds of her vest.

"Which one?" Lafayette asked him. They were both whispering, even though they were completely alone. But the station was so very echoey, it felt like the thing to do.

"All of it, if only in pieces," he said, sounding a little more awake than before. "But especially this one down here, in the south. Past the Mountainous Belt."

"You've been there?" Lafayette asked.

She felt Tristan's head on her shoulder moving as he shook his head. "No, I've just read about it. The bulk of our old records that don't come from this settlement come from there."

"Why that one?" she asked.

But he just shook his head again. "I don't know. But I'd love to find out."

"Put that away," Dieter hissed even before he came into view. He towered over them both, hands on hips like a disappointed dad. Tristan shifted away from Lafayette guiltily, and she thumbed the tablet off again and sat forward so she could slide it back inside her vest pocket.

"My father has maps in his journals," Lafayette said to them both as she struggled to get the tablet into the pocket. She felt Tristan's hand behind her, moving a fold of fabric out of her way. Then he helped her seal up the pocket's closure.

"I have a few rough maps as well," Tristan said. "But mine were copied out of Central Planning approved sources. I would bet your dad actually tried to get to a lot of these places. His maps might be better."

"I need to get into the hidey-hole," Lafayette said.

Dieter blew out an irritated breath. "Of course you do." He pressed his thumb and forefinger to the bridge of his nose like he was trying to fight off a headache. "Look, the first tram will be here soon. And we already don't exactly fit in. No one our age commutes at this hour. So try to behave yourselves, all right?"

Lafayette looked down at her clothes. They had been pretty city-typical and not particularly noticeable. But that had been before she'd gotten all dirty.

Tristan had stayed cleaner, and his university uniform was recognizable.

But Dieter in his street waif gear might be ideal for blending into the shadows in the alleys. But on a tram full of people?

"We'll behave," Lafayette said. Although she was fairly confident she and Tristan weren't going to be the problem.

CHAPTER 18

The station platform was four levels higher than any of the buildings around it, and was, like the bottom level, open on all four sides. So Lafayette could see out to the east. But the lights of the city were too pervasive for her to make out when the sky near the horizon started to lighten.

But she knew it had to be happening when the early morning commuters started trickling in. They came singly and in pairs, yawning and talking only in soft murmurs or not at all. A lot of them looking nearly as worn out already as Tristan was.

A few of the people who sat on the benches near Lafayette and Tristan gave them a second glance, but none of them did more than shrug before carrying on with their own morning routine while waiting for the tram to arrive.

Lafayette was pretty sure none of them were noticing Dieter, who was lurking in the closest thing the well-lit station platform had to shadows.

Lafayette looked at all the people around her, just little glances out of the corners of her eye so no one thought she was staring at them. She wondered where they were all going. In the village, people either had jobs at their homes like weaving or smithing, or they gathered together under the village tree to sort out the work they were doing together, like farming or building new structures.

But these people had other work. Something they had to get up for earlier than they clearly would've liked. And quite a few of them had books, even though they were nowhere near the library or the university. Books were just that commonplace here.

Even more than the preponderance of electric lights, that made it feel like a magical place to Lafayette. She could get used to a place where she was free to read more than the assigned school reader with its very rudimentary language and stilted storytelling.

She was still trying to discern just what was the topic of the nearest woman's book when she caught a blur of motion in the far periphery of her vision.

Dieter was signaling for her and Tristan to get up. She nudged Tristan, and they stood up. Only then did she hear the creaking sounds of a car approaching along one of the cable paths. Dieter herded the two of them close to the edge of the platform before the other commuters started getting to their feet. They were first in line to board, although with everything outside of the station tower still in darkness, Lafayette could not see what they were waiting to board yet.

Then Dieter took something out of his pocket. Lafayette, again as surreptitiously as she could, looked around at the other commuters around them. Many of them already had little metal cards in their hands, cards with a deliberate pattern of holes punched into one side of them. They were holding them with the holes side facing out, ready to be deployed.

She remembered the words of the woman who had sold her the skewers of meat near the gate. So that was what a tramways pass looked like.

But what Dieter had in his hand was not that. It was a very different sort of metal, for one. Not as shiny, not as pure. And the holes punched into it were nowhere near as neatly made. It looked more like someone had poked them out by hand than by machine, using an awl or something similar.

Her stomach started tying into knots, but she didn't dare even try to whisper a question to Dieter. This either worked or it didn't.

She remembered what Tristan said about Dieter's risk assessment abilities, and decided she would just have to have faith.

But that was like practicing patience. It was far from easy. She could hold her tongue, but she couldn't make her stomach stop roiling.

The car rolled up to the very end of the lines of cable it was dangling from, the last few meters of the journey a sharper swoop up until it was hanging level with the edge of the platform. Then the doors opened in the middle of the car. There was a machine standing just where the doors had parted, with room for passengers to step by on either side of it.

Dieter stepped forward with that not-a-pass in his hand. He stuck it into a slot in the machine, but nothing happened. Other commuters were passing on the other side, sticking their passes in and pulling them out again after the light on top turned green and a soft chime sounded.

But nothing was happening with Dieter's pass. Tristan looked like he was about to say something, but Dieter shot him a quick quelling look.

Then he pounded a fist on the top of the machine.

Something must have clicked in place, because the light came on, and the chime sounded. Dieter gestured for Tristan to go past him and the machine to the back of the car as he pulled the pass out, then jammed it in again.

This time he pounded the machine right away, and even before the chime had sounded, he was grabbing Lafayette's elbow and hustling her after Tristan.

Tristan walked with her to the very back of the car and they sat on a narrow bench together. Dieter soon followed, choosing instead to stand in the aisle between their bench and the one next to it. He held onto a pole that came up out of the back of the bench in front of Tristan and Lafayette and turned partway around.

It looked like he was talking with them. Not like he was turning away from the rest of the car. Although Lafayette knew which was the real reason for his choice of position.

The car was only about half-filled when the doors slid shut and they swooped down a steep few meters before settling into a more level path.

Flying over the city.

Lafayette did her best to resist the urge to press her hands and face flat against the glass of the window beside her. But in the early morning light, there wasn't much to see below her anyway.

Still, it was an amazing sight. They were traveling from the south-east part of the city to the north-east part. And since she was on the lefthand side of the car, she could easily make out the lights that glittered all the way up and down the spire. The mini-city on top of it glowed like a crown of diamonds, the lights winking in and out. She was sure it was just the angle of various buildings in that mini-city blocking this or that light as the tram car traveled by at an angle.

And yet, it wasn't hard to imagine that crown of buildings was dancing for her. Throwing her little winks of hello.

"Have you ever been up there?" she whispered to Tristan.

He raised both his eyebrows in surprise. "No one goes up there but Central Planning. I don't think I even *know* anyone who's been up there," he whispered back to her.

"Sure you have," Dieter said in somewhat less of a whisper. "You just don't know you have."

It didn't take long before they were swooping up sharply again, approaching another station platform. Dieter made a small gesture for her to stay in her seat, so Lafayette just leaned back, pressing the tablet between her spine and the back of her seat and tried to look like she belonged while another dozen or so commuters stuck their passes into the machine then dispersed to open seats around the car.

"We're okay," Tristan told her.

And Lafayette realized she was gritting her teeth, her jaw was set so tight. More than that, her entire body was like one big fist, clenched up as tight as her muscles could make it. And he had noticed.

"I feel out of place," she admitted.

"You're with me," he told her, jostling her gently with his shoulder. "And I don't look out of place. You're fine."

She supposed there was some truth in that. His school uniform made him a part of the city in a way anyone could tell with a single glance. If she was close beside him, it was like he was shielding her from attention as well.

Still, she had never truly appreciated how much, even without Kora with her, she felt like she was drawing stares. Even in her new city clothes, she didn't feel like she blended in.

Then she looked up at Dieter, who was holding loosely onto the pole with one hand, letting the motion of the tram car rock him back and forth. His eyes were half-closed, like he was catching a standing up nap.

She would bet anything that he always felt like he was a part of things, no matter where he was. Blending in was his way of life.

"This is it," Dieter said without looking up at either of them or at the station they were approaching.

Lafayette let Tristan take her elbow as they joined a throng of commuters exiting the station at this tower. She wasn't worried about tripping, or about the gap between the side of the car and the edge of the platform. She just wanted to be a little bit closer to the protection of his uniform.

Dieter slid through the crowd like a fish through water. Every single person was *this close* to brushing up against him, and yet, with little twists of his body, no one ever quite touched him.

Lafayette, even with Tristan close beside her, wasn't so lucky. She was jostled all over, mostly by elbows, but occasionally someone closer to her height struck her with a shoulder.

She clutched the tablet all the tighter, nervous that it would be knocked from her grasp. Or that someone would just feel it there, under her vest.

Then they were climbing aboard another tram, Dieter repeating his trick with the fake pass and the quick blows with his fist to the top of the machine.

This car was more crowded than the first, and rather than sit separately next to strangers, Tristan held onto one of the poles with one hand and onto Lafayette with the other. She turned her back to him and leaned against him, keeping the tablet between them. Just in case.

The rocking motion was actually kind of fun. If only she hadn't been so terrified of someone realizing she didn't belong there, that she was smuggling contraband around the city, she might have actually enjoyed this ride.

It took two more changes of tram before they reached the university's own station tower. It was located on a part of the university grounds that Lafayette had never seen before. It took the better part of half an hour of walking before she even saw anything familiar, and longer still before they reached the cafeteria.

The breakfast rush was in full swing, with students lining up at the door. Others who had food already were gathered in groups on the grassy lawn, enjoying the warm morning sunlight as they ate fruit and yogurt or pastries or strips of some kind of jerky.

Lafayette's stomach grumbled loudly, particularly at the spicy smell of the jerky, but there was no stopping until the tablet was safely secured. And maybe not even then. There was so much to do, now that she finally had something that could help her find a way to get her dad out of orbit.

Dieter led the way around the back of the building, down the hill to the back door to the cellar. He knocked on the door, but the worker who opened it to peer out at them was not the woman from the other night. Lafayette chewed at her lip nervously, remembering what Dieter had told her before. Not everyone who worked here was accommodating. Was this guy?

But there was another invisible exchange. Dieter, without even reaching into his pocket, put something into the palm of the kitchen worker. The worker looked at it without opening his hand enough for Lafayette to see what it was.

Then he just shrugged and walked away, leaving the door open behind him.

"Come on," Dieter said, waving for them to hurry in after him.

Lafayette threw one last sweeping glance around the alley. She had, for half a second, felt like someone was watching them. Was Margo about to make another strangely timed appearance? Or was this just Dieter's kids, once more silently watching now that Lafayette had returned to their neighborhood?

But she didn't hesitate in following the others inside. She was digging her key on its ring out of her pocket before they were anywhere near the far end of the storage area, where the hidey-hole was.

But, as it turned out, she didn't need to have her key to get inside the hidey-hole. Because when they reached it, they found the disguised door standing wide open, the hole exposed.

And entirely empty of its contents.

CHAPTER 19

For a minute, Lafayette just stood there. It was like her whole body had gone numb. She couldn't process any thoughts. She couldn't even move.

She was only vaguely aware of Tristan gently extracting the tablet from her nerveless fingers.

But then all of her anger washed over her in a rush, and she spun on Dieter, rising up onto her tiptoes in a vain attempt to get into his face.

"Where are my parents' things?" she demanded. "You came in here and read the journals. So where did you put them?"

"I didn't touch anything," Dieter said. Unlike Tristan with his crimson blushes, Dieter's face went paler when his emotions ran high. He was so pale now she could see the blue of his veins. Particularly the one in his temple that was pounding as he thrust his jaw out at her. "I told you we shouldn't take anything. But you just had to have that. So congratulations. Now it's *all* you have."

"How could anyone know we have this?" Lafayette demanded. She wanted to poke him in the chest with the tablet to underline her point, but Tristan was holding it now. So she just curled her hands into fists and planted them on her hips. "How am I supposed to believe that you don't know anything about this? You, who runs a little gang who keeps an eye on everything? But you want me to believe that the ship saw us take that tablet and sent out… whatever you think came in here, and took all my parents' stuff in retaliation? Their life work?"

Her voice was hitching, and she had to stop talking, stop even looking at Dieter's pale but otherwise emotionless face, until she could calm down enough not to burst into tears.

"Their life work," she said, but more quietly now. "Where is it?"

"Confiscated," Dieter said. It was like he spat out just that one word.

"Confiscated," Tristan repeated. "By Central Planning? But that means…"

He trailed off, his face flushed red with his hazel eyes wide in horror.

But before Lafayette could ask what it meant, she heard something that instantly had her in panic mode.

She heard Kora, barking in the distance. Barking in genuine alarm. Loud and insistent, and tinged with real fear. She could hear the dog part of her and the teacher part of her both in that tinge of fear.

"Uche," Tristan said. Then he thrust the tablet into Dieter's unready hands and turned to run out of the cafeteria.

Lafayette ran after him, but passed him as they headed out the door and up the hill towards Uche's house. As tired as she was, she still had reserves that Tristan lacked.

She could sprint the whole way if she had to. And she had to. Because Kora needed her.

The barking stopped, but all too suddenly. Lafayette was vaguely aware of students in groups around her, whispering together in unease and growing alarm.

Watching her as she ran past them all.

She was about to make the last turn into the alley that led to Uche's house when something hit her from behind. She went sprawling down onto the rough stones of the road, landing first on her knees in a way that felt like her kneecaps were about to shatter, then flat on her stomach. She just avoided biting down on her tongue, but her teeth weren't too happy about the speed at which they impacted each other.

She tried to scramble back up, but there was a weight on her.

No, a person.

She threw back an elbow, but whoever was behind her expected it and grabbed her arm before she could make impact. Then they had her other arm too and were lifting her up off the ground like she weighed nothing at all.

She kicked and fought as she was manhandled into a gap between two buildings. But she only made impact with the backs of her heels a few times, and her new shoes were soft and comfortable.

She wished she had worn her sturdy boots with their thick, heavy soles.

Then she was pushed forward, stumbling into something soft.

Which turned out to be Tristan. He caught her in an embrace and pulled her deeper into the shadows between the houses.

"Quiet," he whispered in her ear urgently. "It will be worse for him if they catch us, too. Understand?"

Lafayette stopped struggling against him. Then she looked back over her shoulder at Dieter behind her.

He was touching the back of his hand to his bleeding, split lip. So she had landed at least one blow from her elbow. Bizarrely—since she knew he had only been trying to help her after all—she was glad she hadn't completely failed at fighting back.

But then Tristan's words sank in.

"Uche?" she whispered.

"They have him now," Dieter said. He was standing half in and half out of the gap between the houses where Tristan was still trying to pull Lafayette deeper into the shadows. But from where Dieter was standing, he probably had a decent enough view of the front of Uche's house.

"You see him?" she asked.

"Yes," Dieter said.

He only said the one word, but it carried so much weight. The tone of his voice, the subtle changes in his body language, all of it spoke volumes.

Uche Okafo was in very deep trouble. Perhaps the worst sort of trouble.

And it was all her fault.

"Maybe they just want to talk to him?" Tristan said with so much tremulous hope in his voice it made Lafayette's heart ache.

"No," was all Dieter said.

"I'll turn myself in," Lafayette said. "You still have the tablet, right? So you can finish the work without me."

"Lafayette, no," Tristan said, clutching at her as if he was afraid she was about to run away.

Which, she totally was.

"You'll only make it worse for him by doing that," Dieter said. He shifted his position to one that was better able to block the exit if she tried to escape. "His only hope is to deny all knowledge of what we've been up to. If you run out there to turn yourself in now, there's no way they'll believe him."

"But if I stay here, they will?" Lafayette asked.

Dieter said nothing. But that vein in his temple throbbed again.

That was definitely a no. It was just the only hope they had.

"Hold onto her," Dieter said to Tristan, and Tristan put both of his arms around Lafayette. But it was less a restraint than a gesture of comfort. Which made it that much harder to break out of somehow.

Lafayette let her body sag against Tristan's and watched dully as Dieter slipped out of the gap between the houses.

And then somehow slipped into shadows despite the morning sun shining directly down the length of that alley. It was less like he was finding shadows than that he was creating them somehow when he needed them.

"Everything is gone," Lafayette said.

"Yes," Tristan said and swallowed hard. "They have your things from the cafeteria cellar already. Now that they've arrested Uche, they're going to empty his house as well. They won't even try to sort contraband from allowed material. They'll just destroy everything."

"But they can't," Lafayette said.

"It's what they do," he told her.

"No, I mean, that makes no sense," Lafayette insisted. "Given how much they know about what we're trying to learn, they have to know what we know already. Right? So they have access to the exact sorts of books we're always looking for. They must. I don't think they're going to destroy anything. I think they're just going to control who can see it. And it's only them who see it."

"Maybe," Tristan said.

"We still have the tablet?" she asked him after a few agonizing seconds of silence between them proved too long for her.

The sounds of the neighborhood going about its normal morning routine were too hard to hear. Like no one else even knew what was happening. She could hear students laughing and talking on the grassy lawn, people in the buildings closer to her cooking breakfast or pounding away at something in a workshop.

"We have the tablet," he said. "But we can't stay."

"In this alley, or in this city?" she asked him.

He barked out a humorless laugh. "Either. But we have to get out of this alley first. Once Dieter is back, we can hide out in my room."

"Won't they look for you there?" Lafayette asked.

"It's not my officially designated dorm room," he said with a fresh rush of color to his cheeks. "I think we'll be okay. Just until the patrols around here lighten up and we can, as you say, get out of the city. We can eat a little and sleep a little and figure out our next step from there. No one will find us."

"Once Dieter is back," Lafayette said, repeating his words. "Where is Dieter? What's he doing that's so important that he left us here waiting for him when there are patrols hunting for us right this minute?"

She knew from the look on Tristan's face that her words had come out far too harsh, although only a little harsher than she had intended them.

Then she heard the soft sound of feet on the cobblestones behind her. But not Dieter. Definitely not Dieter.

First of all, no one heard Dieter moving when he didn't want them to.

But more importantly, it wasn't the sound of two shoe-clad feet behind her. It was four dog paws, the nails clicking ever so slightly against the stone.

"Kora!" Lafayette said, pushing away from Tristan to throw her arms around the dog's neck.

"Lafayette!" Kora said, over and over again. Just like she used to back when it had been the only word she could say.

That had driven Lafayette mad, back in the day. But somehow, in the last few weeks, the sound of her mother's dog saying her name had become the sweetest sound in the world.

"I thought this might be important," Dieter said. There was a strange rigidity to his words, like they were brittle somehow. Although the idea that Dieter could have his feelings hurt by anything Lafayette said was laughable. "But you're not wrong about the patrols. The utility tunnels are not an option."

"I was thinking my place?" Tristan said.

Dieter stood silently for several seconds, thinking this over. Lafayette just struggled to calm the squirmingly happy dog in her arms.

"I thought I'd lost you forever, Lafayette," Kora said. "Uche told me to hide, so I hid, but I didn't know how you'd ever find me. I didn't know where you were!"

"Dieter found you, so it's all right now," Lafayette said to her in as gentle a tone as she could muster. Her own heart was beating so fast.

The feeling of being watched was so strong now. And the sense that, under the normal morning neighborhood sounds, there lurked the rougher sounds of patrols on the hunt.

"Fine," Dieter said at last. "I'll get you there safe and sound. But then I need to see to my people."

"Thank you, Dieter," Tristan said, but Dieter just brushed his words away.

"Dieter?" Lafayette chimed up from where she was still sitting on the ground, holding a barely calmed Kora. "I'm sorry."

The vein in his temple jumped again. But he just gave her a curt nod.

Then he waved for them both to follow him, back out into the sunlit streets.

CHAPTER 20

Dieter led the two of them, plus Kora, through the streets around the university as if they were navigating some sort of labyrinth. Only places where he would abruptly turn them around to backtrack hadn't been dead ends to her eyes. They would just be making their way—as sneakily as they could without looking like they were sneaking—along one road when Dieter would signal for them to turn at once and go back to duck down one of the alleys.

Those alleys were all dead ends, if things like fences or the backs of buildings stopped you. But Dieter didn't see them that way. He just hoisted himself up and over any obstacle.

Lafayette clambered behind him as gracefully as she could. And Dieter was always there to help the less agile Tristan along.

But Lafayette saw the relief in his eyes the instant he realized that Kora, with her hover disc capable of levitating her hundreds of meters into the air if necessary, wasn't going to be a hinderance. It made her belatedly realize that he must have made one of his notorious risk assessments before he'd gone to get Kora.

Whether the risk she carried would be worth rescuing her.

Had he decided her value was worth the potential cost?

Maybe. But something in the level of relief that flashed through his dark eyes told Lafayette the truth might well be a little different.

She was pretty sure he had decided the risks bringing Kora with them introduced were absolutely not worth it.

And then he'd went and gotten her from wherever she was hiding, anyway.

Not that Lafayette had even a second to thank him. Or thought that he'd do anything besides wave her words away. But she definitely owed him something. The minute she had the chance to give it to him.

She never saw a patrol. Tristan had described their uniforms to her, that what looked like padded, heavy garments were really some kind of armor. That they dressed all in black with tall, shiny boots. That they wore hats, usually with the bills pulled low over their eyes. That they wore no name tags or insignia like the patrolling law enforcement out in the villages always did, but that you knew you were in real trouble when you encountered one whose armored uniform was red and not black.

She never saw even a glimpse of such a uniform. But from time to time she was absolutely sure what she was hearing were their boots on the cobblestone roads, always drawing closer without ever quite closing in.

She also never saw who was watching their progress. Although she knew without question that eyes were always on them. From rooftops or alleys, from doorways or windows. There was a network all around them, keeping tabs on their progress.

And, from the suddenness of their turn-arounds, maybe even somehow signaling to Dieter what they knew about the lay of the land.

After a long night's walk across the city, and especially all those stairs, spending the morning at high alert but still on the move was brutally exhausting. Her adrenaline was so high she couldn't stop her hands from shaking. But they were never reaching a moment's safety where she could try to calm her panic down. They just had to keep moving. They only stopped when the danger was higher than walking, definitely not a moment to relax.

They were always one bad turn away from getting caught. She

knew it. She didn't need to see the tight clenching of Dieter's jaw to know he didn't think they were safe at all.

Then she sensed Tristan's entire body sag in sudden relieved relaxation and realized they had finally reached their destination.

It was almost like the hidey-hole door in the back of the cellar, a door disguised as part of the stonework of the outer wall of a tower. Which was a particular trick, as this tower was round. The door had a curve to it. And after Dieter had it open, Lafayette saw it wasn't just covered with something to make it look like stone. It actually was built from blocks of stone. The edges of the door were jagged, matching the offset rows of the stone blocks.

Tristan ran ahead, up a flight of wooden spiral stairs and into a darkness overhead. Kora zipped up after him, not even pretending not to use her hover disc.

But Lafayette lingered at the doorway where Dieter still stood.

The door was set up off the ground on some sort of metal contraption, like a gate. When she looked to where there should be hinges, she saw motors inside the wall. So that was how Dieter had gotten it open despite the weight. There was a combination of mechanical and electrical components at work in that system. She wanted to get a better look at it.

But Dieter apparently thought she was lingering there for other reasons.

"Go on up," he told her, gripping her arm to gently guide her inside the tower. And out of the light that gave her the best view of what was holding that door open. "I'll be back when I can. Just stay with Tristan. He'll keep you safe." Then he chuckled as if to himself and added, "Or maybe vice versa. Anyway, look after each other."

"Where are you going?" Lafayette asked.

"To get your tablet, for one," he said.

Which was the first time Lafayette noticed neither he nor Tristan had been carrying it all through their circuitous travels through the neighborhood, with all the climbing and backtracking. The last time she had seen it, Tristan had had it.

No, that wasn't right. Tristan had thrust it at Dieter before running to Uche's house.

"It's still in the cafeteria?" Lafayette asked. She didn't want to sound accusing. But she knew she did.

"No, it's safe," he told her, deliberately not reacting to her tone. But then he clutched her arm again. He hesitated for a moment, like he didn't know what was going to happen after that clutch. His fingers were hot like brands against her arm, even with the thin, draping cloth of her vest between his skin and hers.

Then he was pushing her away from him, in towards the stairs. "Go."

He was outside now, sliding the door shut again. All of that stone was moving into place between them, blocking out the sun. She just managed to get out a quick, "Be safe!"

Then the door closed with a thud that carried far too much finality for her.

She wasn't even sure if he had heard her.

She ran up the stairs. So many stairs, around and around, with no landings and no doorways until she reached the very top of the tower. She could see the underside of the round, pyramidical cap of the top of the tower above her as she opened the simple wooden door at the top of the last step.

And ducked under the surprisingly low lintel into a long, narrow, windowless space. A few dim electric lanterns were glowing, but they seemed to cast more shadows than light. The support beams overhead were heavy and thick, running from the top of the ceiling on her right scarcely taller than the top of her head down to the floor on her left.

The entire space was one deep equilateral triangle. There was furniture inside: a cot with the bedding in disarray, a desk cluttered with papers and books, and several tables even more cluttered than that desk. But with the floor space on the lefthand side of the room mostly unusable due to the angle of the ceiling, most of the floor was covered in stacks of books as well.

"You and Uche have a lot in common," Lafayette said without thinking.

It was like her words, but especially Uche's name, fell out of her mouth to hit the floor with a crash.

Tristan was turning on another pair of lanterns on a table at the very far end of the room. She saw his back stiffen, but then relax as if by force of will. Only then did he turn to her, his face unsmiling.

"Yeah," was all he said. "Most of these are his books, too. I guess this is all that's left of his personal library now."

"I'm so sorry," Lafayette said.

"For what?" Tristan shot back. "For wanting to help your dad? For, frankly, wanting to do the work of history? The work Central Planning won't let us do? I don't think there's anything to be sorry for in any of that. And I *know* Uche didn't think so either."

"I'm sorry this is happening," Lafayette said.

"Yeah, me too," Tristan said, his anger gone as suddenly as it had appeared.

"So no one knows you live here?" she asked.

"Above the library? Nope," he said with a shrug.

"We're in the library?"

Clearly, she had lost track of all those twists and turns. But she should've recognized where they were even as they sneaked in through the back of the building. What other building had she seen with capped towers?

"Uche knew about this place," Tristan said. "This is where he was hiding what he didn't want Central Planning to know he had. My actual dorm is another thirty minutes of walking south of here, close to the station we were at this morning, actually. I got tired of all the walking, so one night I just started using the cot that was already here. I haven't been to my dorm room in weeks. My roommate must think I'm dead, or that I dropped out."

"What are you going to do now?" Lafayette asked.

"The same as your parents, I guess," he said glumly, standing with his hands in his pockets and looking out over the stacks and stacks of books. Like he was wistful for all the things he would never now have time to read.

She knew how he felt.

"Drop out?" she said. "Do you have to? Maybe they don't know you were even involved."

"No," he said with a sad shake of his head. "It was always unlikely, that I would get all the way to the end of the history program and actually receive a degree. My family doesn't have the Central Planning connections to smooth my way, and I haven't been like some of the other students, obviously cravenly seeking their approval. I swear, half the students in the history program are only there because they're hoping to find someone they can report, for their own gain."

"Where do you think Uche is now?" Lafayette asked. She looked around for a place to sit, but aside from the rather uncomfortable looking chair that was drawn up to the desk, the only place was the cot or the floor.

"Uche?" Tristan said even as he slumped down onto his cot, sitting on it crosswise with his back against the wall. He gestured for her to join him. Lafayette slipped off her shoes, saw her socks were little cleaner and peeled them off as well, then sat down next to him.

In a flash, Kora was up on the bed beside her, curling up against the side of her leg with her tail curled around Lafayette's hip and her chin resting on Lafayette's knee. The dog seemed to go to sleep at once, and Lafayette was a little jealous of that.

She was bone tired. But she didn't see any restful sleep in her future.

Still, she rested her head against Tristan's shoulder. Like he had done to hers back in the station.

"Yes, Uche," she said. "Where would they take him?"

"No one knows," he said, tipping his head so that it was lying against the top of hers. Then he adjusted a little, getting the pouf of her hair bun out of the way before resting his head against hers again. "No one who is taken by Central Planning ever comes back."

"Maybe he's in the city on top of the ship," Lafayette said.

"Maybe," Tristan said. "Rumor has it that there's a secret island, out on the Watery Sea, only accessible by Central Planning somehow. Once they take you there, you stay there until the day you die."

"Is this a rumor like the rumor about how the spire in the center of the city is actually the remains of a ship from space?" Lafayette asked. She wanted to inject a little humor into her tone, to take the edge off the sad reality they were discussing. But she couldn't quite do it.

"Maybe," Tristan said. He sounded like he was half asleep again, drifting away from her.

"Maybe the island you don't come back from is the mini-city, then," Lafayette said. Although she supposed planning a daring raid to rescue Uche would have to wait until Dieter was back.

"Or," Tristan said, "there really is an island, and then there are rumors there is an island, so people think the rumors can't possibly be true." He sighed. "Uche was working on a book, you know. About Central Planning, their history and how they work. And one of the things that kept coming up over and over again, but that absolutely couldn't even be hinted at in his book, was how they use stories. They write their own versions of things, so close to reality in most regards and yet absolutely far away where it suits them to lie. And then their versions mingle with the truth, until no one can tell one from the other anymore."

"Because they have all the books," Lafayette said. She wasn't willing to let go of her theory, that they weren't destroying everything but hoarding it.

Because if they were hoarding it, all of it could be liberated again.

But if they truly were destroying it?

Lafayette couldn't even dwell on those thoughts.

There was a vibrating sound, momentarily alarming before Lafayette realized it was just Kora, snoring as she dozed against Lafayette's thigh.

And then that snore was matched by a softer sound from Tristan.

That, plus the stifling warmth of the windowless room, was too soporific even for Lafayette's anxious mind.

She wanted to plan. She wanted to figure out a way to pack up and get all the books around them to some safer place.

But her eyelids were getting heavier and heavier.

She had one last thought, about where the tablet they had risked everything for was now.

And then she drifted away into exhausted sleep.

CHAPTER 21

Lafayette woke some time later to a gentle rustling sound. Kora was still pressed against her, snoring. But somehow, instead of sitting with her back to the wall, Lafayette was lying down on that cot with Kora curled up against her tummy, her head on Lafayette's arm. And there was a blanket over the two of them that definitely hadn't been there before.

As if anyone could need a blanket in such a warm room. But it was a kind gesture all the same.

Lafayette opened her eyes to see Tristan sitting cross-legged on the floor with his back to her. He was not two meters away from her, sifting through a stack of loose papers. He regarded each sheet in turn, then placed it on either a short stack by his right knee or a taller, sloppier stack by his left.

"What're you doing?" Lafayette asked, her words slurring together as she extricated her brain out of its sleeping state and back into wakefulness.

"I was looking at maps," he told her. "The versions I had in my journal weren't great. But I have the source material here, mostly. If I can remember where I put them all."

"Maps, plural?" Lafayette asked, sitting up onto her elbow. Kora groaned in protest at the motion, but didn't quite wake up.

Tristan turned to look over his shoulder at her. "I think some of these were your dad's," he said.

Lafayette gently slid out from behind Kora, crawling around her to get off the cot without jostling her. Then she crouched behind Tristan to look at the map he was currently holding.

"Yeah. That's definitely his hand," she said. "But the details are off from the ones he had in his journals."

That brought a lump to her throat. His journals, which were all gone now. Either destroyed or hidden away in some secret library she would never, ever have access to. She'd never see them again.

She pushed those wailing thoughts to the back of her mind with an almost audible grunt of effort and focused on what was in front of them.

"He would've drawn these based on what he could find in books here in the city," Tristan said. "The ones in his journal were from later. After he'd seen at least some of these places he marked here."

He pointed to a few soft Xs drawn on the map.

"You're right," Lafayette said. "That's where he started looking for the crater, although it was a lot farther south and west than that. And this X over here? That's the village where he thought everyone who walked away from the crash ended up settling. Or, most of them, anyway."

"Right," Tristan said. "But the ship in the crater is in space now. And the village?"

"Is just a village," Lafayette said. But then she pointed to the northernmost X. "That's where we have to go."

"You're sure?" Tristan asked.

"The one under the sea? Forget about it," she said. "Although taken together with the rumors of this prison island, it does make me wonder."

"That maybe the island is actually a ship? Interesting. But trying to find it is going to call for resources we just don't have," Tristan said. "And the same with this southern one, beyond the mountains."

"If only we had a dirigible," Lafayette sighed. "Don't you have those here in the city?"

She had herself yet to see one as anything other than a drawing in a book. She knew Central Planning used them to move goods and occasionally people around. But even they mostly traveled over the roads in caravans these days.

"The mountains are too tall for a dirigible to get over," Tristan told her.

"Seriously?" Lafayette asked.

"Seriously," he said. "The air gets too thin, I think. Or the prevailing winds are too strong. Something like that. Anyway, they can't."

Lafayette thought of the principles of physics book she hadn't made much of a dent in. Gone now. Along with her own journals. And absolutely everything else.

"They aren't safe over this much water either," Tristan went on, pointing at the map and deliberately not noticing the hitching in Lafayette's breath. For which she was grateful.

"Can dirigibles go north?" she asked when she could trust her voice to work again. "Does the air get thin there too?"

"It gets cold," he said. "Very cold. But I think they work. I don't actually know. The place marked on the map is a lot further north than the northernmost settlement. I'm not sure if anyone has even tried to fly that far north."

"Not that it matters," Lafayette said. "Where are we going to get a dirigible?"

"My family doesn't have one," Tristan said lightly. But if that was a joke, Lafayette wasn't sure she quite got it. "Um, we're one of the wealthiest families in the city. We've been transporting goods for generations," he explained.

"I'll have to walk, then," she said with a sigh, and shifted from squatting on her heels to sitting on the floor.

Even as Tristan turned his cross-legged pose around to face her.

"What are you talking about?" he asked her.

"Well, obviously, that's the only way to help my dad now. I don't think I can get up to that city on top of the spire. I wouldn't even know how to start trying. But walking north until there is no more north to walk to? I can do that."

She wanted to add the word "easily," but couldn't quite do it. She knew the map wasn't to scale. But it was close enough to tell that the walking she was committing herself to doing was four times the distance she had gone already since leaving her hometown.

And without her father's camping equipment. Or even her own reliable boots. Because Central Planning had taken all of her stuff.

"No, I mean, what do you mean 'I'?" Tristan said, putting a hand on her knee. "We're going together. I thought you knew that."

"I can't ask you to do that," she said.

"I guess I missed the part where you were asking," he said with a hint of his old, lopsided grin. "I mean, I'm volunteering. And not just to help you. This ship, if we can find it, is a major discovery. It could make my career."

"The career you're walking away from by dropping out of university?" Lafayette reminded him.

"Yeah. Like your dad," he said. "Although credit due to your dad, he found his ship first."

"He found all of them first," Lafayette said. "These are his maps. It's all his writing. I had no idea he had left so much behind here in the city."

"Well, he left in a hurry," Tristan said. "Just like I'm about to. Look, if Dieter doesn't get here soon, we're going to have to clear out, anyway. I don't want to get caught here. I don't want to lead people here."

"Yeah, I guess it's way too much to try to pack up and move," Lafayette said. Although she was so tempted to try. "But if we leave—"

"Dieter will find us anyway," Tristan assured her. "Central Planning has nothing on his network, I promise you."

Lafayette had no trouble believing that. But it prompted a lot of uncomfortable questions in her mind.

"Are we making the right choice?" she found herself asking out loud even as the thought rose in her mind.

"What do you mean?" he asked.

"I want to help my dad," she said. "And I think I need to get to that ship to do it. Or, at least, I'm really, really hoping that's going to help."

"I know," he said. But he was still looking at her with that eager, curious look on his face. Like hearing her voice was all he wanted in the world in this moment.

It was a lot, the rush of feelings she was getting just from one look. She felt her own cheeks heating up, although she hoped on her it was less apparent than it always was on his pale skin.

"The thing is, there's helping my dad, and then there's helping everyone," she said.

He frowned a little, but didn't interrupt.

"I mean, Central Planning is empirically terrible. Right? And shouldn't people know that?"

"I think they do," Tristan said. But he wasn't grinning now. He was as serious as she was.

"Shouldn't they know it better, then?" she said. "Shouldn't they know what we know?"

"Here's the thing. We can't prove what we know," he said. "And more than that, as much as everything that Central Planning says is largely lies, because they control everything their lies are things they can *prove*. It's an ugly situation. But I promise you, if there was a way to resolve it in the name of truth, Uche Okafo would've found it. Your father would've found it."

"My father chose not to try," Lafayette said. "And I think Uche, in his own way, chose not to as well."

"Okay," Tristan said.

They both noticed in that moment that his hand was still on her knee from before. But he didn't move it, and she didn't brush it away.

"Okay," he said again, his voice a little deeper than before. More solemn. "So what you're asking is what we're going to choose. Right?"

"Right," she said.

"I think we have to choose to save your dad," he said.

For some reason, that answer made Lafayette's shoulders slump. It was everything she had wanted to hear, really. But hearing it, she hated how badly she had wanted it. Like she was being selfish.

But helping *everyone* felt like more than she could do.

There *was* no good answer. That was the problem.

"Listen," Tristan said. "If we save your dad, that's the moment.

That's when we'll have all the proof we can ever possibly need to show everyone the lies Central Planning has been forcing them to swallow for so many years."

"You want my dad to be some kind of crusader?" Lafayette asked. Which wasn't the craziest thought in the world. It wasn't remotely the work he preferred doing, which was being alone in the wilderness, making slow, tedious progress towards uncovering the smallest possible bits of the truth.

But she could see him choosing to take up the mantle. If she asked him to.

But Tristan was shaking his head. "I mean, maybe? But what I meant was, when we bring his ship down, we can make sure everyone sees it. Just because we go north to figure things out doesn't mean that's where he has to land."

"We can land his ship right here in the city," Lafayette said, finally understanding what he was driving at.

"Or, you know, just outside of it," he said.

And then he did grin at her.

And she smiled back at him. She was feeling warmer now, in a way that had little to do with the stifling air under the library rafters.

The hand on her knee flexed a little, giving her thigh a little squeeze. And for a moment, it felt like she and Tristan were sort of drifting closer to each other.

But before Lafayette quite knew what was happening, Kora was bolt upright on the cot, barking for all she was worth.

Lafayette lunged for her shoes, but Tristan was already halfway to the door.

He didn't get a chance to get any closer, though. Not before it thumped open with a bang.

For an instant, Lafayette was ready to laugh away her alarm as silly paranoia. Because framed in that doorway was Dieter. Why he wanted to make a dramatic entrance on this of all days was beyond her, but whatever.

Only she saw the look on his face. Like he was sorry about something. Banging the door, maybe? But the idea that he could ever look apologetic about anything was alarming all on its own.

And then she saw the guards in their black, armored uniforms standing on the stairs behind him. And she knew they were too late. Their chance to escape the city was gone now.

They were in the clutches of Central Planning.

CHAPTER 22

Lafayette dropped her shoes and lunged at Dieter. She had a vague plan that involved shoving him and the two guards behind him down the stairs, then slamming that door closed behind them.

And nothing beyond that. No thought as to how she, Kora, and Tristan would get out of the windowless room after she'd barricaded the only door. Which she was sure was like Uche's and had no lock.

But she never got the chance to even try. Because her feet slipped on the wet floor where her socks were. She caught herself without falling and resumed her charge, but that split second of delay was all Dieter needed. He stepped forward, caught her in his arms, and spun her out of the way as the two guards behind him came into the room.

She became a flailing mass of elbows and heels, battering him as he held her up off the ground with his arms locked around her waist. She knew she hit him more than once. She heard him grunt, even over the sound of Kora's ceaseless barking.

But he didn't let her go.

"Get a crate for the animal," one of the guards shouted down the stairs even as the other advanced on Kora, still standing on the cot and barking for all she was worth.

"Kora, run away!" Lafayette shrieked. The dog had a chance. She could use her hover disc. She could zip down the stairs as fast as a bird, slip past the other guards, get out into the open.

And then what? All of Lafayette's plans were nothing more than first steps, where the second steps were bound to be infinitely harder to pull off than the already impossible first ones.

Then four more guards came into the room, carrying empty totes. The speed with which they filled them with books and papers and hauled them back down the stairs made it clear they had done this before. They had done it often enough to get very efficient with it.

"The boss is on her way up," someone yelled from the bottom of the stairs. "Shackle the prisoners, then give me an all clear."

Another guard came into the room with a crate that looked like a cage, a single door in one end that latched shut. A cage just large enough to hold Kora.

Although it took a bit of work for the two of them to shove the dog in there. And even then, Lafayette could tell they only really succeeded because Kora was too overwhelmed to fight them. She was howling now, howling in a way that sounded like it longed to be articulate. Like she wanted more than anything to be calling out Lafayette's name. But even in her panic, she was remembering herself.

"Don't hurt her," Lafayette said to Dieter.

"I'm not in charge here," he said to her. Even as he set her down on her feet so that the guard approaching with the restraints could fasten them around her wrists.

"You must have some sway," Lafayette insisted. She hated the bite when the cord-like restraints pressed into her flesh, so tight her wrist bones were grinding against each other. It felt so... final.

"Hold out your wrists," the guard said.

Lafayette was about to point out that her wrists were already bound when Dieter gently pushed her to one side to thrust his own hands out at the guard.

"What's going on?" Lafayette asked Dieter as the restraints were hissed tight around his wrists. If anything, his looked tighter than hers.

"We're being detained," he told her. "Anything that happens after this is as much a mystery to me as it is to you."

"But you opted not to fight it?" Lafayette asked incredulously.

Dieter just looked at her. But whatever was going on in those dark eyes, she couldn't glean it. He just looked down at her, like he was memorizing every feature of her face.

Like he didn't think he'd ever see it again.

"Why aren't you fighting?" she asked him in the lowest of whispers. But he didn't answer.

"All clear," someone yelled, and Lafayette looked over to see Tristan was restrained as well. He looked down at his own wrists with a blank look on his face, like he couldn't quite believe any of this was real.

Footsteps echoed up the spiral staircase, then a silhouette blocked the door. A woman, by the suggestions of her body shape through the padded armor of her guard uniform. Although her uniform was different from the others, more of a deep magma shade of red than their all-over black.

An officer. She was the boss. She was in charge.

The woman paused in the doorway for a moment with her head down, the bill of her cap covering her face. Then she lifted her chin, and Lafayette fought the urge to swear out loud.

It was Margo Weiss.

But her bright smile, less friendly and more triumphant now as she threw gloating looks at Dieter and Lafayette, wavered when she saw Tristan there as well, deeper in the room.

"Oh," she said. It was strange how such a small word, such a soft sound, could carry so much meaning. But she lifted her chin once more and the look of sad disappointment on her face was gone as quickly as it had appeared. "I suppose there was no way you weren't involved in all this. You practically live in Uche Okafo's house, and you are studying under him. Still, I had hoped it was just the riff-raff hoarding the contraband and you were somehow unaware of how they were using you." She tipped her head to one side and shrugged in a way that was clearly meant to project her complete lack of emotional involvement in any of it. "Oh well."

Tristan said nothing. He was very pale, and his eyes still had that numb look to them.

"She found your things first," Dieter said to Lafayette. He wasn't whispering. But maybe they were past any hope of keeping secrets. She tried to ignore him, but he pressed on. "She followed us to the cafeteria that night. That's why she was there. And she broke in and took all of your things. And with that as a probable cause, she directed the guards to bring in Uche Okafo. You led them right to him."

Lafayette bit down hard on her lip. The pain was the only thing that was keeping her from crying.

But when Dieter repeated his first statement with heavier tones of accusation, "She found your things first," Lafayette snapped around to stare right into his eyes.

They were so unreadable. But she was sure she was right. He wasn't accusing her of causing Uche's downfall. He was pretending to be angry and accusing her of being to blame, but that wasn't what his fierce gaze was trying to tell her.

He was trying to tell her that none of these guards knew anything about the tablet.

The tablet she still didn't know the current location of. Only that he had said it was safe.

Lafayette glared up at him, hoping if she projected as much anger as he was sending her way, he would see it as her telling him she'd gotten his message.

Tristan tried to move to stand between them, as if they weren't all restrained and he needed to head off a fight between them before it got physical. But the guard near him stopped him with a hand on his arm.

Margo just chuckled. "Children, children. No fighting. You all broke the law together, so you'll all go down together. No sense turning on each other now."

"Yeah, we should've done it days ago, when it could've meant something," Dieter sneered at her.

But Margo just barked out another laugh. "Yes, perhaps. But tattlers tend to go down in the end as well. It's hard to wash the stink of traitor off your skin once you brush up against it."

"Why?" Lafayette asked her. She had a lot of questions for Margo, but they all started with that one word. Why.

"She doesn't want to tell you why," Dieter said, leaning forward as if to whisper conspiratorially in Lafayette's ear. But he didn't deign to whisper. He just glared up at Margo over Lafayette's shoulder as he spoke. "She wants to tell you how. She's dying to brag on the how."

"I don't brag," Margo said with a toss of her head. Like she'd forgotten she was wearing a hat, and her wave of hair was firmly held back under it. "I don't have to brag. I've earned my place now. I'm going upstairs, to Central Planning proper. No more night shifts at the library, or endless rotations through the homes of retired professors. I get to really help now."

"That's kind of her why," Tristan said. "It's not really about us. Or Uche. Or doing what's right."

But Lafayette felt the heat from Dieter's breath as he hovered there, too close to her. He wanted something from her.

He had suggested Margo wanted to brag. Was he trying to get her to help him play for time?

It was a desperate hope. But it was all Lafayette had.

She licked her lips, looked into the face of the young woman she had come so close to hoping would be her friend, and said, "How?"

Margo reached into her pocket and pulled out something she held in her closed hand. She lifted it to Lafayette's eye level, then opened her hand.

Resting on her palm was an exact duplicate of Lafayette's key. Not the ring, just the key. As much as, with her hands so painfully bound together, she couldn't touch her pocket to assure herself it was still there, she was pretty sure she could feel it digging into her hip.

"So many outfits," Margo said with what had once seemed like such a bright, friendly smile. It was the same smile, but the context had completely changed. It made Lafayette feel cold now. And like something slimy was on her skin.

"I had my back turned to you more than once while I was changing," Lafayette said. "You made a copy?"

"Trivially easy," she said. "I already knew where the hidden room was, of course. I could've reported that to Central Planning days ago. But the team who responded, who broke down that door and liberated your contraband, they would've taken all the credit. So I had to find another way. A way that ended with me rolling a wheelbarrow of contraband into the guard office myself and turning it in to the section chief. No one could steal the credit from me then."

"Good for you," Lafayette said dully.

"*Very* good for me," Margo said. "I knew you were trouble the minute I met you, with that strange dog always at your heels. But I had no idea. I still can't believe my luck. The things you have in those journals! I earned so much credit with Central Planning I don't even have to start out at the lowest rank when I go upstairs. I get to jump two ranks before I even start my first day of work. And that means this much nicer uniform. So thanks."

"And such lovely work it will be," Dieter said.

Margo shot him a quelling look. Then she gestured to the other guards in the room. "Bring them all downstairs. The wagons are arriving that will transport them to the spire."

"What about Kora?" Lafayette asked. "She's coming with us, right?"

"Kora," Margo said with a wrinkle of distaste to her nose, as if that were scarcely an appropriate name for a dog, "is contraband. She's going in the wagon with the rest of the contraband. Well, I mean, the contraband that isn't going straight onto the bonfire."

"Bonfire," Tristan said, but dully. Like he wasn't entirely awake.

But Lafayette already knew Margo wasn't lying. From her position closer to the door, she could smell smoke on the air. And it wasn't cooking smoke she was smelling, or the greener smell she knew from burning fallow fields from her village back home.

No, this was the smell of burning paper. And book binding. And leather covers.

This was the smell of knowledge going up in flames.

Margo gave a few more orders before striding out of the room. The guards carrying Kora between them in the cage passed next, and Lafayette tried to reach out towards the dog, but a guard she didn't even know was standing behind her gripped her shoulder so tightly it hurt, keeping her in place.

Then he shoved her, equally as needlessly aggressively, towards the stairs.

She heard Dieter being marched behind her, and assumed Tristan would follow. There was little left in the room now, save the furniture.

All the books and papers had disappeared even as they were all talking.

When she emerged at the bottom of the stairs and was marched out the tower door, she saw that fire for herself. It was roaring hot, so hot she could feel her skin start to burn even from the considerable distance away she was.

And two guards in protective suits were still adding books to that fire.

So much for her hope of a secret library. All the knowledge really was about to be gone. And her parents' journals and hers as well were already ash now.

All she had left was what she held in her head. For as long as they let her keep that.

Someone stepped up beside her, and she glanced over, expecting maybe Dieter but more likely Tristan joining her in her moment of grief.

But it was Margo, watching the flames dance in the full light of the afternoon sun.

"Pity," Margo said, as if continuing a conversation Lafayette didn't remember having. She turned her back to the fire, but leaned closer to Lafayette's face to add, "Imagine if you'd just told me you were all in on being a botanist. There was just a smidge of a chance I would've believed you. I could've pinned this all on your filthy street friend. You would've been safe. Tristan would've been safe. But alas. You wanted to be coy. So, congratulations."

Then she was gone. Lafayette blinked back tears, as much from the stinging presence of book ash that filled the air as from emotion.

But then it was Dieter leaning closer to her to say, "It was always going to end this way for her. She was always going to use you to advance her own position. Don't believe her when she says otherwise."

She looked up at him, trying to blink the ash away and really wishing she could use her hands to wipe at them. Although maybe that would just make things worse.

But Dieter was looking at her oddly. It was a smile of sorts, not his usual smirk, but a cousin.

"What?" she demanded.

"Don't thank me yet," he said.

She hadn't been about to. But rather than pointing that out, she snapped, "Why not?"

His grin just deepened a couple of degrees before he said, "Because now is too soon. Give it a minute."

"What happens in a minute?" Lafayette asked.

But the guard at her shoulder just shoved her hard again, starting the process of herding her towards the waiting wagon.

She had no choice but to stumble in the direction he was shoving her, but when she had a chance to throw a glance back, she did so.

Dieter was still grinning. Even as his body flowed effortlessly around the attempts of his own guard to shove him like Lafayette was being shoved, he kept grinning.

He was walking to the same fate as she was. So what did he find so delightful about all of this?

And why did she have the sudden overwhelming urge to grin as well?

CHAPTER 23

There were two wagons parked side by side in the middle of the street that ran alongside the library. Beyond them, Lafayette could see the grassy lawn of the plaza in front of the library. It was filled with students soaking up the warmth of the afternoon, giggling together and breaking into runs as they realized they were going to be late for their next class.

She had never seen a group of people work so hard not to notice what was happening nearby. But she could tell they were doing just that. The laughter sounded forced. Their steps all quickened at the same point when things down this street would just come into meaningful view.

Their eyes were too studiously not drawn to the flames filling the intersection behind her.

The wagons were heaving up and down ever so slightly, like they were really beasts of burden breathing heavily as they waited to be loaded up and not machines. But Lafayette had traveled with the caravan long enough to know what that motion meant.

The engines were running. They were ready to roll. The minute the three of them were on board, they would be gone. The library would be a distant memory behind them.

And she had no idea what happened after that. She didn't think Tristan or Dieter did, either.

She could hear Kora barking and whining in panic and alarm, and she longed to go to her. But Kora was in the back of one wagon, and the guard behind her was driving Lafayette to the other wagon.

Then Margo was suddenly there again, walking briskly past Lafayette and her guard. She didn't slow her pace, just tossed back over her shoulder. "The burn squad is moving out. Get these three to the spire and I'll meet you there."

"Yes, sir," her guard said, even as Lafayette heard the roar of more wagon engines. The other wagons behind her, filled with the guards who had carried all the books and papers down from the attic room to the bonfire in the street, were leaving. Their job was done. Only two guards remained to watch over the fire and presumably keep the flames from spreading to the surrounding buildings.

Because they didn't want *approved* books to burn, did they?

Lafayette bit back the hysterical urge to laugh and turned her attention back to the wagon ahead of her.

She couldn't see inside of it. The door was standing open, but the interior was all inky blackness.

And she was about to be thrust into it.

Suddenly there was a sound, louder than the students laughing up ahead in the plaza and louder than the crackling of the fire behind her. Perhaps it was louder only because it was all around her. She wasn't sure. But it was like the sound of a sudden rain of heavy drops pounding hard into the ground. It reminded her of her time in the jungle, where a sudden cloudburst of hard rain was pretty much a daily occurrence.

It was only when the guard behind her fell to the ground at her feet that she realized what she was hearing wasn't rain.

It was rocks.

She shrieked, throwing her arms over her head even as she finally saw the cascade of stones she had been hearing. They were as thick as any rain, pounding on the exposed back of the guard who had been so eager to hurt her as he herded her around. He didn't so much as move despite that pounding, though.

Probably because of the sizable lump on his temple where the skin was split and bleeding. He was clearly unconscious now.

Just like the jungle rain, the rain of stones ended as suddenly as it had begun. But when Lafayette uncovered her head to look around, it was to find that only the guards had fallen under that hail of stones.

She, Dieter, and Tristan were all standing, still restrained and Dieter with the split lip she had given him earlier, but other than that, totally unharmed.

"Diet?" Tristan said almost plaintively. Like he really hoped this was somehow Dieter's doing and not some new horrible situation they were getting swept up in.

"Sorry I couldn't save your books, but it wasn't safe to even try this until the burn squad moved out," Dieter said. He twisted his hands in some kind of spinning gesture, like part of a dance that ended with his arms spread wide.

No longer restrained. The broken remains lay at his feet. But he quickly stepped over them to reach Lafayette. He dug down into her pocket, ignoring her yelp of protest, and came out with her multitool. She had totally forgotten it was still there.

But he just grinned at her, stepping away to turn his attention to Tristan's restraints first. It took one snip of the multitool to break them apart.

"Kora," Lafayette said, even as Dieter came over to finally cut her free.

"Got her," Tristan said, and dove into the back of the wagon where Kora was still whining. She gave a sharp bark of surprise and joy.

And then she was bounding out of the wagon, jumping all over Lafayette. Dieter snipped her restraints free, then put the multitool back into Lafayette's pocket. But Lafayette just dropped to her knees and let Kora jump all over her.

"We have to get out of here," Tristan said.

"Obviously," Dieter said, and raised a hand. He made a series of signals to no one Lafayette could see.

"These guys aren't dead. They're just out of it," Lafayette said from where she was still on her knees. Her hands might be busy rubbing all over Kora's wiggling body, but that low vantage point was enough to see that every guard near her was still breathing. If shallowly.

"Can we get to Uche?" Tristan asked.

"I wouldn't even know how to start," Dieter said. "We have to get hidden now. Margo is going to notice we're not following, and knowing her, she'll notice it long before she gets to the spire."

"Where to?" Lafayette asked, getting to her feet.

Her bare feet. Her shoes were still upstairs somewhere. Or maybe in the fire.

"Underground, eventually," Dieter said. "Nothing Kora can't handle. Right, girl?"

"Dieter!" Kora said, and wagged her tail.

But rather than going down the street or to one of the darker alleys off the main street, Dieter led them straight back into the library tower. The stone door was still standing open as the guards had left it.

He didn't lead them back up the stairs, though. He ducked down under the lowest steps of the spiraling staircase into what had to be, at best, a crawl space.

But when Lafayette and Kora plunged in after him, she saw him disappearing down a hatch. A hatch that, when closed, would line up exactly with the pattern of the wide wood planks of the floor. A hidden door.

They were going down another ladder into darkness. And this was just as gritty, cold, and slimy as the other. Only this time, it wasn't just her hands touching that mess. It was her feet as well.

Her feet wanted to slide so much she had to curl her toes to grip the rungs as she descended.

But when she got to the bottom, she felt Dieter's hands on her hips, helping her down. He kept her hoisted up, setting her down behind him where the floor was drier, if still cold and gritty.

Tristan came last, having spent a moment struggling with the hatch to get it closed behind them. He landed deftly enough just outside the borders of that puddle.

"Explain again how rain causes these puddles?" Lafayette said. Because rain collecting at the bottom of a ladder that was itself at the bottom of a staircase completely encased in stone was a little hard to grasp.

But Dieter just grinned at her.

"I want to know how you got caught and why you let them force you to lead them to us," Tristan said.

Dieter's face sobered at once. "I had to. I had to buy my brother and sister time to get away. And my sister has the tablet, so I didn't think you'd argue with my decision later."

"We don't even know if the tablet is worth anything, let alone all this," Lafayette said. "Uche getting arrested might have happened anyway, but leading them to us to save the tablet meant so many books and papers getting destroyed. They're not replaceable."

But Tristan just said, "Brother and sister?"

And Dieter grinned again. "Come on. Time to meet my family," he said, throwing an arm around each of their shoulders.

"Your family," she repeated. "I thought you were an orphan."

"Why would you think that?" he asked, although the persistence of his grin said he knew full well he preferred people to think that about him. "I mean, you've met my two younger siblings already."

"I have?" she repeated.

But Tristan chuckled dryly. "Oh, sure. I should've seen the resemblance."

Lafayette cast back in her memory for anyone she had seen with the same features as Dieter. But that was a little hard to pin down. His clothing choices were clearly designed to be a distraction from actually seeing *him*. And so was his posture, making him appear as waifish and thin when he was wiry and muscled.

His brown hair was all too common, and while the hairstyle might be unique, that sort of thing tended not to run in families.

His eyes were unique as well, and that *could* run in families.

But then she remembered what had struck her most about his eyes when they'd first met. That familiar sense, like she knew what it felt like to be watched by him.

And it clicked in her head. Those two kids, the ones that had helped her move the wheelbarrow of totes and journals to the kitchen. They had a similar way of just watching her.

"Those kids," she said. Which wasn't particularly specific, but Dieter nodded anyway.

"My brother Archer and my sister Finley," Dieter said.

"So you're the oldest," Lafayette said.

Which made Dieter laugh again. "Not remotely," he said. "I'm third from the bottom, but I'm sixth from the top."

"You have nine siblings?" Tristan said, and even in the dark, Lafayette could hear the sound of his feet stumbling as he walked.

So he hadn't known either. And he'd known Dieter far longer than she had.

"All the times you would talk about your people, I thought you meant the other kids in your street gang," Tristan said.

"He kind of did," Lafayette said.

"My people means both my blood family and my fellow people living on the fringes of this society," Dieter said. "I protect them all. Even if it means lying by omission to my best friend, who's as close as a brother to me. And I have five of those, so I know what that means."

"Your parents?" Lafayette prompted.

But all the laughter went out of Dieter. "A story for another time," was all he would say. "Come on. Let's pick up the pace. We need to get there before they're gone."

"Gone? Gone where?" Tristan asked.

"Thanks to all the attention we've been drawing, it isn't safe for anyone down here anymore," Dieter said. He sounded bitter, but Lafayette was pretty sure that wasn't directed at her. He didn't blame her. Like he kept telling her, he blamed Central Planning.

"But there's a whole community down here," Tristan said.

"Couple hundred people," Dieter agreed. "We aren't moving out all in one clump, though. No worries. We've had contingency plans for this for decades. And we've practiced the steps. It's sooner than we hoped, this move, but later than we feared. It'll be okay."

"But where is everyone going?" Lafayette asked.

"A lot of us already travel with the caravans for part of the year, so that will just be full-time for a while," Dieter said.

"Your family are traders?" she asked.

"No, but a lot of the others down here are. My family, we have other skills," he said. "My siblings are staying in the city. Not down here. This place is as burnt to us as the remains of Uche's personal library. But in other out-of-the-way places. They'll be fine."

"They? Not you?" Lafayette asked.

"Of course not me," Dieter said, and threw that jolly arm around her shoulders again to give her a rather too aggressive side hug. "I'm going to the far north with you guys. You didn't think I'd loan you the family dirigible without piloting it myself, did you?"

"We're doing what now?" Tristan asked weakly.

"We're going north," Dieter tossed back to him. "We have a ship to find and Lafayette's father to save. But first we have to get to that dirigible. We launch at dusk."

"And how long have you been planning this?" Lafayette asked him.

"Well, leaving by dirigible has always been one of our escape plans," he told her. "But the north as our destination? Only since you pointed to it on a map at the tram station."

Which he had been nowhere around when she had done that. He just knew. Because of course he did.

"Just like that, you're going?" she asked.

"Just like that, we're all three going," he said. Then he added, "And Kora!"

And Kora barked out a happy, "Dieter!"

And really, how could Lafayette argue with that?

CHAPTER 24

Their walk ended in another large underground chamber filled with crates stacked on top of pallets to keep them off the floor. But it wasn't the same chamber as before. Lafayette had a decent mental map going, and despite being underground with only her gut sense to rely on for directions, she knew they weren't in the same place as the night before.

That was south and west of where they were now. She'd swear it. They'd left the library in a direction that was more straight across the city to the south than in towards the spire.

Although, all things considered, maybe she wouldn't want to swear to it. It had been a rough night. More, a rough couple of days.

The crates had an abandoned feel to them, their sides showing signs of mold growth. There was certainly no sense of being watched. And although globes of light burst suddenly into full brilliance at their approach, there was no sign of any people there with them.

Then Dieter called out, "All clear!" And like magic, two young men were suddenly standing in front of them. They had their arms crossed, as if they had been waiting there for quite some time. But Lafayette knew they hadn't been there when the lights had first come on.

"Your brothers," she said. It wasn't a question.

"Two of them," Dieter said, then gestured towards them one at a time. "This is Karlo, and this is Till. Don't worry if you get them confused. They aren't really twins, they just like to be interchangeable with each other."

"Funny," Karlo said, raising a single eyebrow at Dieter. Both of the older brothers were dressed more like the commuters from the tram ride that morning than Dieter or the two youngest siblings. But they had to be in their mid twenties, a little past the age to pass oneself off as an urchin.

But blending in by looking like a random city worker? They had that down cold.

"Everyone else is out?" Dieter asked.

"On the way," Karlo said, tossing a glance at Till, who just nodded without saying a word.

"And the dirigible?" Dieter asked.

"You have a heading for where you're going?" Karlo asked, adjusting his crossed arms to be sure his big brother disapproval of Dieter's plans was clear.

"We have a general sense," Dieter said. "All the maps just went up in flames. But it's fine. We'd already worked out that none of them were entirely accurate. And Finley has the tablet, which is all we really need."

"Finley has the tablet?" Lafayette said, the words bursting out of her. "Where is she?"

"Around," Karlo said, but not like he was being vague to put her off. No, from the way his gaze drifted around the mountains of crates surrounding them, he knew she was there somewhere. He just didn't know where, specifically.

"She'll bring it to you," Dieter assured her. "I told her to source some blank books for the two of you first, so you can restart your journals on the way north. It's going to be a lot of boring days of travel before we get to a point where a map would even be helpful. And by then you'll have remembered enough to get us started. Right?"

He added the last with somewhat less confidence than he had said all the rest. But Lafayette hurried to nod at him. "Sure. A blank page and a pen and hours of time. That's all I need."

"I remember things as well," Kora put in, wagging her tail as she looked up at Dieter. Lafayette felt a stab that took her a second to identify as jealousy. But it's not like she could be mad. Dieter had, at least twice in the last few hours, saved Kora's life. Of course, the dog now loved him to pieces.

But Karlo said in a wavering voice, "Did that robot dog just… talk?"

"She does that," Lafayette said.

"She has a construct," Tristan said. "That's part of our ancestors' technology, kind of like a ghost—"

But Karlo was already raising both of his hands as if in surrender. "I'm sure it's a long story. And I know you can tell it well, from what Dieter tells me. But we don't have the time to get into it. We have to get you safely gone from here, for all our sakes."

"What about Uche?" Tristan said. "I mean, I know we can't really do anything for him. But it feels like the wrong thing to do, just leaving him here at the mercy of Central Planning."

"He was playing up the sick old man routine," someone said, and Lafayette turned to see one of Dieter's younger siblings standing behind her with a stack of fresh-looking journals as well as the engineering intern's tablet.

"Finley?" Lafayette guessed.

"Yeah," Finley said, although with her gravelly voice and short haircut, it was a little hard to identify her as a girl, even though Dieter had said she was his sister. Lafayette would just have to take his word for it. "Here," Finley said, shoving the stack of books and the tablet into Lafayette's arms.

"What were you saying about Uche?" Tristan asked her.

"You know that thing he does where he pretends to be shaky and weak?" Finley said. As if she had ever had eyes inside Uche's house to see him when he wasn't pretending at frailty.

But Tristan just nodded.

"He was doing it when they arrested him, but a lot more," Finley said. "He was asking for compassionate treatment. And that girl Margo Weiss said if he cooperated, he would get it."

"A lie," Dieter said.

But Finley shrugged. "I read her as sincere."

To Lafayette's surprise, Dieter seemed to take this assessment seriously. Even though it contradicted everything he had ever said about Margo. He just looked at his sister and said, "You sure?"

And Finley said, "Yes. She's ambitious, but she also truly cares about Uche's wellbeing. If she can help him at all, she will. I mean, she was very concerned that she got all the credit for the raid—"

"So she could get her promotion," Lafayette said.

"—so her orders would be followed as to the treatment of Uche," Finley said, talking right over Lafayette.

"Finley isn't often wrong about people," Dieter told Lafayette. "I mean, I don't think I am, either. But if the two of us differ in our sense of what someone else really wants, I guess I'd have to admit she's always been the one who turned out to be right."

Finley said nothing. But the smugness she was radiating was definitely a family trait.

"So catch me up," Tristan said, rubbing at his face tiredly. "Margo was suspicious of Lafayette from the moment she arrived in the city. And she followed us to the cafeteria, found a way to steal Lafayette's key and cleared out everything we had stashed there so she could bring it in herself rather than merely reporting its existence to the authorities. But she did that just to earn a high enough rank to make sure that when Uche was detained, he was treated well?"

"She didn't steal my key, she just copied it," Lafayette said.

"But otherwise, yeah," Dieter said. "It sounds like maybe that was her plan. If Finley is right. Which she generally is."

"So what happens to Uche now?" Tristan asked.

"He'll be detained for a time before they decide what to do with him," Karlo said. "And if they decide he needs medical treatment, he will go to the hospital upstairs."

"That means in what you call the mini-city," Dieter told Lafayette, who just nodded at him, annoyed he was interrupting to explain something that was perfectly clear in context.

"It's possible he stays in the hospital once he gets there," Karlo went on. "It's not unheard of. And it certainly is the closest thing we'll get to a decent opportunity to get him out of there."

"Wait, you're going to rescue him?" Tristan asked. He was clutching his hands together, like he was afraid to hope too much.

And the look Karlo shot his way clearly said it was important to calibrate his expectations. "We'll do all we can, Till and I. A lot of it is going to depend on what Uche does. And we won't be able to communicate with him what we need him to do. It'll be tricky."

Till said nothing, just gave the smallest of nods in agreement.

"And there's nothing we can do to help with that?" Tristan asked.

"We're going to the north," Dieter told him. "That's how we help."

"In the north?" Tristan said doubtfully.

But even before Karlo could speak, Lafayette felt sure she knew what he was going to say. So she got there first. "By getting as far from the city as possible," she said.

"Exactly," Karlo said. Then his face grew grave, almost sad. "I know your story, a little. Your family's story a little more. I'm sorry we're meeting under these circumstances. We were still watching you and trying to come to a decision about how to approach you when all this happened."

"Dieter was supposed to keep you out of trouble," Finley said, almost with the singsong tone of a tattle-tale.

Dieter scowled at her. "Dieter tried," he said.

"So," Karlo said, slapping his hands together as if to forestall an argument that only an older brother could see coming. "We've been busy since we talked earlier. The dirigible is airworthy and ready to launch. We have stores being put onboard even now. Everything you said you needed, plus a few thing Till and I think you might've missed asking for. Food, warm clothes, gear for traveling over snow when you get there."

"Snow," Lafayette said. She knew what it was. She had just never thought she'd see it for herself in her lifetime.

"Snow and ice," Karlo said. "I hope you three are prepared for whatever lies up there. It's not a place sane people go by choice, you know. If this is really where a fifth of our ancestors came down, they definitely either died there, or they came south and never went north again. Because the north is a terrible place."

"I thought my answers were all here, in the capital city," Lafayette said. "But all I found was trouble. It's actually a relief, knowing that where I'm going next is as far as I can get from civilization."

"But not alone this time," Tristan said.

"No," she agreed. "Not alone."

"We will do all we can for Uche while you are away," Karlo told her. "You just rescue your dad. Because when you bring that ship down, you'll be rescuing us all."

"I hope that's true," Lafayette said.

"Do we have shoes for Lafayette?" Dieter asked, and Finley nodded and ran into the maze of crates. Then he turned to Lafayette and Tristan, and that old familiar grin was back on his face. "So, you guys got a quick nap in while I was arranging all this, right? Now you're ready for more walking? Only we have to get to the far end of the city before nightfall, so it's going to be more of a jog."

Tristan made a sound like he was biting back a groan, but nodded all the same.

Kora was looking from Dieter to Lafayette, her tail wagging like mad. Like she was waiting for her now two favorite people to join hands or something.

Lafayette wasn't feeling quite that warmly towards Dieter. But even so, it was nice to be heading out on a journey with companions this time. She couldn't help answering his grin with a smile of her own, even as she stepped closer to Tristan and grasped his hand, intertwining his fingers with hers.

More long hours of walking felt almost impossible, tired as she was and as beat as Tristan looked. But with companionship, she was finding, even the most difficult of tasks somehow felt… doable.

They were going to make it to the dirigible on time. And then they were going to reach the north and find that ship.

And then, then she'd finally find a way to rescue her dad.

It was all doable now. Not even Central Planning could stop her.

She was on her way.

CHECK OUT BOOK THREE

History sleeps beneath them all, and she will wake it.

Lafayette Eloi stole something incredibly precious. Something she knows her government would kill to keep under their protection. No, under their control.

She stole knowledge. Knowledge of the past of all her people.

She got away with it, thanks to her new friends in the capital city. Tristan Carey knows more about the world than Lafayette ever knew existed. And Dieter Bohm brings the most crucial element of all.

His family owns a dirigible. With that, their plan to reach the Arctic regions in the far north becomes just barely possible.

The government chases hot on their heels. And the resources at their command eclipse anything Lafayette and her friends can muster.

Lafayette will never quit. Her only hope for a future lies in uncovering the past. And sharing all she learns with her entire planet. No matter what the price.

Salvaging the Arctic Wreck (Available September 9, 2025 direct from me or October 14, 2025 in stores everywhere.)

SCI-FI SERIAL PODCAST!

Check out my new monthly podcast of serialized science fiction: THE TALES OF THE CHAI MAKHANI TRIO!

Elyot loathes the massive Commonwealth ships that hover menacingly over his home world of Adghal. He hates the Commonwealth enforcers who harass the populace even more. But with his mother missing and presumed dead, Elyot keeps his head down and strives to avoid notice. And he succeeds until the day two strangers enter his life...

New episodes of this sci-fi serial drop every 1st of the month.

Now streaming on Apple Podcasts, Google Podcasts, Spotify, Stitcher and more. Also available in eBook and print everywhere books or sold. For a complete episode listing, check out the page on my website.

COMPLETE SERIES: THE TRAVELS OF SCOUT SHANNON

The complete six-book series THE TRAVELS OF SCOUT SHANNON begin with book one, Under Falling Skies.

Scout Shannon's whole family died the day the Space Farers dropped an asteroid on their domed city. Now she lives alone, out in the wild with only her dogs for company. She prefers it that way.

But Scout finds herself at a crossroads. One road leads back to a quiet life snug under the protective dome of a city. The other road leads to a life in the rebellion, a life of adventure and excitement but also danger. Dare she try to find the rebels hiding in the hills?

Then a chance encounter with a stranger from the other side of the galaxy threatens to derail what remains of Scout's life. The entire galaxy awaits her, if she survives the next four days.

"Under Falling Skies", a young adult science fiction novel, set on a remote planet with a distinctly Old West feel. For fans of gunslinging women and young girl assassins. And dogs.

Under Falling Skies, the first book in THE TRAVELS OF SCOUT SHANNON, available everywhere now.

COMPLETE SERIES: THE RITCHIE AND FITZ SCI-FI MURDER MYSTERIES

The Ritchie and Fitz Sci-Fi Murder Mysteries starts with Murder on the Intergalactic Railway.

For Murdina Ritchie, acceptance at the Oymyakon Foreign Service Academy means one last chance at her dream of becoming a diplomat for the Union of Free Worlds. For Shackleton Fitz IV, it represents his last chance not to fail out of military service entirely.

Strange that fate should throw them together now, among the last group of students admitted after the start of the semester. They had once shared the strongest of friendships. But that all ended a long time ago.

But when an insufferable but politically important woman turns up murdered, the two agree to put their differences aside and work together to solve the case.

Because the murderer might strike again. But more importantly, solving a murder would just have to impress the dour colonel who clearly thinks neither of them belong at his academy.

Murder on the Intergalactic Railway, the first book in the Ritchie and Fitz Sci-Fi Murder Mysteries.

ALSO FROM KATE MACLEOD

Love heists and capers? Then check out my new series, THE VIC HARPER CAPERS. The action starts with the novella THE THIRD POLE JOB.

Vic Harper and her gang retired wealthy from their life of thievery and heists. Whether in a luxury condo overlooking the river in Minneapolis or in a modernist mansion built into the side of a mountain in Colorado, life comes easy now.

Perhaps too easy.

When an old friend asks for a favor his niece, Vic and her mentor Chase Woodward leap at the chance to relieve a little of the boredom. But a quick bit of B&E in a wealthy suburb of Chicago leads to an even greater challenge.

The prize? Nothing much. Just the opportunity to level a playing field for their friend's niece.

But the heist? May prove to be their toughest ever. Because to get to the prize, they'll have to climb a mountain.

And not just any mountain. Their prize waits on the summit of Mount Everest.

THE THIRD POLE JOB, the first novella in the Vic Harper Caper series. For those who love capers, heists and other impossible missions.

ALSO FROM RATATOSKR PRESS

Also from Ratatoskr Press, The Witches Three Cozy Mystery Series by Cate Martin, a mix of mystery and magic that begins with Book 1: Charm School.

Amanda Clarke thinks of herself as perfectly ordinary in every way. Just a small-town girl who serves breakfast all day in a little diner nestled next to the highway, nothing but dairy farms for miles around. She fits in there.

But then an old woman she never met dies, and Amanda was named in her will. Now Amanda packs a bag and heads to the big city, to Miss Zenobia Weekes' Charm School for Exceptional Young Ladies. And it's not in just any neighborhood. No, she finds herself on Summit Avenue in St. Paul, a street lined with gorgeous old houses, the former homes of lumber barons, railroad millionaires, even the writer F. Scott Fitzgerald. Why, Amanda can practically hear the jazz music still playing across the decades.

Scratch that. The music really, literally, still plays in the backyard of the charm school. Because the house stretches across time itself. Without a witch to protect this tear in the fabric of the world, anything can spill over. Like music.

Or like murder.

The complete series is out now, and it all starts with Charm School.

FREE EBOOK!

Like exclusive, free content?

To get two prequel short stories to THE RITCHIE AND FITZ SCI-FI MURDER MYSTERIES as well as a bonus prequel novelette to the completed six-book series THE TRAVELS OF SCOUT SHANNON, signup for my monthly newsletter at KateMacLeodWrites.com.

Thank you!

ABOUT THE AUTHOR

Kate MacLeod has written stories which have appeared in Analog, Strange Horizons and Mythic Delirium, among other places. She is also the author of two young adult science fictions series: The Travels of Scout Shannon, and The Ritchie and Fitz Sci-Fi Murder Mysteries. She also contributes to a serialized science fiction podcast called The Tales of the Chai Makhani Trio. She currently lives in Minneapolis, Minnesota.

Find out more about the author and sign up for her newsletter at KateMacLeodWrites.com.

ALSO BY KATE MACLEOD

Novels

The Slums of the Solar System:

Mitwa

The Mars of Malcontents

The Whole World for Each

Books 1-3 Box Set

The Travels of Scout Shannon:

Under Falling Skies

In Quaking Hills

Among Treacherous Stars

Against Impassable Barriers

Over Freezing Altitudes

At Galactic Central

The Travels of Scout Shannon Books 1-3

The Travels of Scout Shannon Books 4-6

The Travels of Scout Shannon Books 1-6

The Ritchie and Fitz Sci-Fi Murder Mysteries:

Murder on the Intergalactic Railway

Murder in the Skies

Body in the Catacombs

Death on the Summit

An Undiplomatic Murder

A Lethal Betrayal

The Forgotten Planet:

Raiding the Forgotten Derelict

Plundering the Planetary Secrets (Available March 11, 2025 direct from me or April 15, 2025 in stores everywhere.)

Sci-Fi Novellas

The Intergenerational Tree

I Rise into a Daybreak

Caper Novellas

The Third Pole Job

The Twelve Days of Christmas Job

10-Story Collections

Tales of Blood and Ink

Tales of Old Gods and New

5-Story Collections

Tales from Heian-Kyo and Others

Tales from the Edges and Ends

Tales from Forgotten Days

Tales from Ancient and Future Times